jazz off-key

Other books in the growing Faithgirlz!™ library

The Faithgirlz! Bible
NIV Faithgirlz! Backpack Bible
My Faithgirlz! Journal

The Blog On Series

Grace Notes (Book One)
Love, Annie (Book Two)
Just Jazz (Book Three)
Storm Rising (Book Four)
Grace Under Pressure (Book Five)
Upsetting Annie (Book Six)
Storm Warning (Book Eight)

The Sophie Series

Sophie's World (Book One)
Sophie's Secret (Book Two)
Sophie and the Scoundrels (Book Three)
Sophie's Irish Showdown (Book Four)
Sophie's First Dance? (Book Five)
Sophie's Stormy Summer (Book Six)
Sophie Breaks the Code (Book Seven)
Sophie Tracks a Thief (Book Eight)
Sophie Flakes Out (Book Nine)
Sophie Loves Jimmy (Book Ten)
Sophie Loses the Lead (Book Eleven)
Sophie's Encore (Book Twelve)

Nonfiction

No Boys Allowed: Devotions for Girls
Girlz Rock: Devotions for You
Chick Chat: More Devotions for Girls
Shine On, Girl!: Devotions to Keep You Sparkling

Check out www.faithgirlz.com

faiThGirLz!™

jazz off-key

DANDI DALEY MACKALL

Requests for information should be addressed to:
Zonderkidz, *Grand Rapids, Michigan 49530*

Library of Congress Cataloging-in-Publication Data

Mackall, Dandi Daley.
Jazz Off-Key / by Dandi Daley Mackall.
p. cm. -- (Blog on series ; bk. 7) (Faithgirlz!)
Summary: Jazz is thrilled at the chance for her own one-woman art show during Big Lake's Spring Fling celebration, but when her younger sister ruins the paintings she had planned to display Jazz rages at family and friends while wishing she could find peace through Jesus.
ISBN-13: 978-0-310-71265-7 (softcover)
ISBN-10: 0-310-71265-3 (softcover)
[1. Artists--Fiction. 2. Anger--Fiction. 3. Down syndrome--Fiction. 4. People with mental disabilities--Fiction. 5. Interpersonal relations--Fiction. 6. Christian life--Fiction.] I. Title.
PZ7.M1905 Jaz 2007
[Fic]--dc22

2007017939

Editor: Barbara Scott
Art direction: Laura Maitner-Mason
Illustrator: Julie Speer
Cover design: Karen Phillips
Interior design: Pamela J.L. Eicher

Illustrations used in this book were created in Adobe Illustrator.
The body text for this book is set in Cochin Medium.

Printed in the United States of America

07 08 09 10 11 12 13 14 • 14 13 12 11 10 9 8 7 6 5 4 3 2 1

So we fix our eyes not on what is seen, but on what is unseen.
For what is seen is temporary, but what is unseen is eternal.

—2 Corinthians 4:18

1

Jasmine Fletcher dipped her brush into the color she'd invented, "grownck" — a mixture of gray, brown, and black — and applied the final touch to her latest masterpiece. It had taken her all month, but she'd finally created a textured abstract that captured the smell of the school cafeteria. She called it Hot Lunch.

All she had left to do was sign her painting. She traded to a fine-point brush, chose grownck, and painted the letters: "J-A-Z — "

"Jasmine?" The knock and door opening struck at the exact same moment, the moment of her signing *Jazz*. The last *Z* jerked and slid like a lightning bolt down the side of her painting.

"It's ruined!" she cried, frantically reaching for a paint rag. She felt, rather than saw, the presence of her mother behind her.

"Jasmine, I'm not your answering service."

"How could you be? You don't wait for answers. You just barge on in," Jazz muttered, dabbing at the stray streak of paint. She'd caught it before it dried, so the damage wasn't too bad. She could fix it.

"What did you say, Jasmine? Don't mumble."

Jazz didn't feel like getting into it with her mother. They'd been at each other more than usual lately, and the whole week of Easter break stretched in front of them. She wiped off the last bit of paint, wadded her rag, and turned to face her mother.

Tosha Fletcher was synonymous with style and sophistication. She wore a tailored pinstripe skirt and jacket, and her hair curved magically into a knot at the base of her neck. Jazz's hair waved and curled at all angles, and that was the way she liked it. Her mother, of course, hated it.

"Did you want something?" Jazz asked, trying to control her voice.

"I want you to take care of your own business and let me conduct mine."

"That's what I was doing... until I was so rudely interrupted." Jazz knew as soon as the words were out of her mouth that they were fighting words. But she couldn't take them back now, even if she wanted to.

"Interrupted?" Mom's dark eyes narrowed. The skin around her jaw tightened. "Let me tell you about interrupted. That's the fourth call from that man. Foley? Or whatever his name is."

"Farley." If she'd really talked to him four times, she should have gotten his name straight, Jazz thought. For once, she kept her thoughts to herself.

"I have work to do, Jasmine. I can't spend the entire weekend fielding phone calls for my daughter. I've left messages all over the house for you to call him back. Why haven't you?"

Jazz had seen the notes. She just hadn't gotten the nerve to call him back. A month earlier she'd practically twisted his arm to get him to hang one of her paintings in his gallery. "Gallery" wasn't exactly the right word for Mr. Farley's shop.

He sold frames and craft kits and how-to booklets, along with a few prints.

"Well? Why haven't you called him back? Apparently, he's going to keep calling until you do. What does he want?"

"You're the one who talked to him. Didn't he tell you?" But Jazz felt pretty sure she knew why he was calling. That was why she kept putting off calling him back. When Mr. Farley had agreed to hang her painting in his store, he'd given the experiment one month. The month was up. It was time for her to take back her painting. She'd really had high hopes of selling it too.

"Jasmine, don't take that tone with me." Her mother took in a deep breath.

Jazz started to defend herself. Then instead, she turned her back on her mother and stuck her brushes into the cleaning jar. "Mr. Farley just wants me to pick up my painting."

"Then go pick it up."

Jazz sloshed her brushes in the jar and watched the clear liquid take on the tint of grownck.

"Now, Jasmine! Before that man calls here again."

Jazz sighed. "All right." She might as well get it over with. Besides, any creative juices had dried up under the piercing glare of her mother.

Jazz stepped out of her house into sunshine that surprised her. In Big Lake, Ohio, the sun went into hibernation sometime in October and, with rare and coveted exceptions, didn't show its face again until May. Yet here it was only the second week in April, and Jazz found herself squinting at the intense sunlight.

"Heads up!" Ty shouted.

Jazz knew her little brother well enough to assume there was a ball headed for her. She ducked just as the baseball whizzed by. "Ty!" she cried.

"Sorry about that," Ty said, walking up the sidewalk, his leather mitt in hand.

Mick, or Michaela, Ty's best buddy, also a seventh grader, jogged up from the opposite direction. She wore jeans and a Cleveland Indians shirt and cap. "Jazz! Are you okay?" She slid off her glove and tossed the ball back to Ty.

"I hear there's a great ball field at the park. No windows. No innocent bystanders." Jazz tried to soften her words with a smile, but she was too wound from her latest mother encounter.

Mick glanced at Ty. "Want to go to the park?"

"Sure."

Mick looked at her watch. "We've got almost two hours." She grinned at Jazz. "See you at noon."

Jazz had almost forgotten about the blog meeting. She and some friends ran a website called *That's What You Think!* The others blogged. Jazz drew cartoons. Mick was webmaster. Two hours would give her plenty of time to pick up her painting at Farley's Frames, bring it home, and still whip up a cartoon for this week's blog.

She started down the jonquil-lined sidewalk. The gardener had planted clusters of red tulips closer to the house. Jazz inhaled the sweet scent of blossoms and buds. She complained a lot about the show-off grandeur of The Fletcher Estate, but on mornings like this it was hard not to enjoy the cultivated grounds. Two mourning doves called back and forth, their soulful notes reminding Jazz of the whistle sound she and Ty used to make by blowing into their folded hands.

As she turned toward town, she gazed up at the blue sky through tree limbs dotted with pale green. The view helped her unclench, slow down. She could see God here. Feel God in the sun on her face and the cool breeze reaching inside her jacket. Hear God in the honking of geese in the distance. Smell God in the new life of spring all around her. Jazz had tried hard not to believe in God. It had only been a couple of months ago when she'd given in and admitted to herself that the world must have been created. And the Master Creator, the Artist, was God.

Since coming to the realization that there really was a Creator God, Jazz had experienced moments like this, times when she sensed God's presence. She was grateful for these brief windows to God in the middle of her crazy life. It made her wish she could have God all the time — not just when she felt touched by nature.

By the time Jazz reached Farley's Frames on Main, her little window of peace was a thing of the past. She'd had to wait forever to get across Highway 42. A couple of idiotic guys gave her a hard time when she cut through Big Lake College. And a minivan splashed her as she crossed Main Street.

Jazz paused outside the shop and collected her thoughts. A month wasn't very long to hang a painting in a gallery. So what if nobody had bought her painting? Was that any reason to yank it off the wall and make her take it back home? People had to get used to seeing original art in Farley's store. That took time. If she could just convince Mr. Farley to leave the painting where it was for another month, maybe a buyer would turn up.

Determined to make Farley see the light, Jazz marched up the steps and into the little shop. Although she used to visit Farley's Frames every day, lately, she'd only gone in on shipment days when he got in prints from New York. She liked to be the first to go through them.

Over half of the store was dedicated to Mr. Farley's frame business. On the back wall partial frames were displayed like nestling Ls. Bins of prints and craft packets took the center of the store.

Jazz's painting had the best spot in the shop, high over the checkout counter, where every paying customer had to look at it, like it or not. Farley, knowing his clientele, had asked Jazz for something realistic or impressionistic, rather than abstract. Jazz had given him the impressionistic painting she'd done of Storm Novelo, one of her friends on the blog team. Storm was mestiza, part Mayan and part Spanish, and Jazz had painted her in the spirit of her ancestors, suggesting a tribal village in the background. Jazz would have preferred giving Mr. Farley one of her abstracts, but the painting of Storm didn't look half bad displayed against the beige wall with dark rafters above.

"Admiring your own work?" Mr. Farley always startled Jazz a little bit. He was tall, bone thin, with deep-set, hollow eyes that would have looked right at home in a skeleton. "I was about to give up on you, Jasmine."

"Sorry, Mr. Farley. I've been busy. Painting and all. I know why you've been calling, and — "

"You do?"

"But it's only been a month, and that's not very long in the art world." Jazz was talking fast. She wanted to get in her whole argument for keeping her painting on display.

"Yes. That's what I wanted to talk to you about."

"But would it be such a big deal to keep the painting where it is for another month? A lot of artists have to wait years to be discovered. A month isn't long! How many customers do you even have in here in a month?"

Mr. Farley opened his mouth to answer, but Jazz cut him off.

"What else would you put there? I mean, my painting has as good a chance of selling as another Norman Rockwell or some of those motel-wall paintings of ships and flowers you hang around here. How many still-life vases can one store handle? Besides, what about promoting the arts? Isn't it your civic duty or something? I'll bet there's a big tax deduction you can take for leaving my painting up." Jazz's mother was very big on tax deductions.

"Wait a minute, Jasmine."

"Mr. Farley, please!" Jazz tried to rein in her desperation, but it was morphing into anger and she couldn't stop it. "Thirty more days! That's all I'm asking! One lousy spot on your whole stinking wall? Why can't you — ?"

"Jasmine Fletcher!" Mr. Farley shouted. Jazz had never heard the man speak above a whisper. She stopped in midsentence. "I'm agreeing with you, Jasmine. I fully intend to keep your painting displayed."

"You do?"

"That's what I've been trying to tell you. It's true that nobody has purchased the painting. But there has been interest."

"There has? Interest? In my painting?"

"What I'd like to do is increase visibility."

Jazz didn't get it. "Increase what?"

"Big Lake is having its Spring Fling celebration next weekend."

Jazz and her family never joined in, but she knew the town had a big Easter-egg hunt and a pancake breakfast put on by the Lion's Club. "I don't — "

"I'd like to have an open house Friday evening. And I want to display your work. Jasmine, how would you like to have your own one-woman art show?"

2

"Don't tell me Jasmine Fletcher is speechless." Mr. Farley smiled down at Jazz, showing teeth the color of yellow ochre.

Still, it was a great smile. A terrific smile. Jazz didn't know if she'd ever seen such a glorious smile. "You ... are you ... you're serious?"

For as long as she could remember, Jazz had dreamed about having a one-woman art show. When her friends were daydreaming about getting married or becoming rock stars, Jazz had imagined having her own art show, watching people as they studied her artwork, listening to them talk about *her,* the artist.

"Quite serious," Mr. Farley replied. "I'll need more paintings, of course. Perhaps half a dozen? I'll be showing the latest prints and collections from New York. But you're the featured artist, Jasmine. That is, if you agree."

"If I agree? Are you kidding? Yes! I agree!"

"Then I'd like those paintings as soon as you can get them to me. I'll keep them back until the opening on Friday evening. I'll alert the press, of course."

"The press?" Jazz imagined her abstract, *Hot Lunch,* on the front page of the *Big Lake News.*

Mr. Farley ran over details with her. She nodded, but everything sailed over her head. She, Jazz Fletcher, was going to have her own art exhibition.

Jazz couldn't wait to tell somebody. She jogged all the way home, waving to the university guys who whistled at her as she cut through campus, dodging traffic on Highway 42. She was hoping Mick and Ty would still be playing ball at the house. Then she remembered she'd as much as ordered them to the park.

She ran on inside. "Hey! Is anybody home?"

Footsteps sounded on the stairs. "Hi, Jasmine!" From the top of the winding stairs Kendra gave her parade wave, her chubby hands moving back and forth like windshield wipers. She was thirteen, a year younger than Jazz, a year older than Ty. If she'd stayed in public school, Kendra would have been in eighth grade. She attended a special school for kids with Down syndrome.

"Kendra! Guess what!" Jazz dashed to the bottom of the stairs.

"Ummm ... You got a puppy?" Kendra guessed.

Jazz laughed. Kendra could always make her laugh. Who better to share her good news with? "Not a puppy. But it's something I've wanted as much as you've wanted a puppy."

"A horse?"

"Not a horse. Okay. Are you ready for this?"

Kendra had come down two steps. Now she stopped and nodded yes. "What?"

"I'm going to have my own art exhibit!" Jazz exclaimed. "A one-woman show!"

"Ya-a-a-ay!" Kendra squealed. She grabbed onto the banister and hobbled down the rest of the stairs, planting both feet firmly on each step before moving to the next. On the bottom step she let go of the banister, held out her arms, and jumped to Jazz.

Jazz had to scramble to stay on her feet. Kendra outweighed her by at least twenty pounds. She hugged her sister, who kept cheering. Kendra's hair smelled like strawberries. "Thanks, honey."

Kendra stopped cheering. "What's a zibbit?"

Jazz tried not to laugh. "An *exhibit* is a show. I get to show off my paintings at Farley's Frames next weekend."

This brought another round of cheers from Kendra.

"Want to help me pick which pieces to put in the show?"

Kendra followed Jazz to the art studio. A few months earlier, Jazz's parents had reluctantly agreed to let her turn the room, formerly the second guest bedroom, into Jazz's own art studio. Now it was her favorite room in the house. She'd painted the walls white and taken down the curtains. The lighting was terrific. And the only furniture in the room consisted of easels, a stool, a table for sculpting, and trays for paints and supplies.

"Which pictures do we get to choose from?" Kendra asked.

Jazz pulled out three canvases from the closet and set them up, leaning them against the wall. Next, she lined up the two easels with her works in progress. "Not much of a choice, huh?" She would have had four more canvases, but a few weeks ago in a fit of temper and doubt, she'd destroyed them. Before that, she'd been concentrating on her sculpting and experimenting with different mediums.

Jazz stepped back from her paintings and took a good look. Two were abstracts, but she was pretty sure Mr. Farley would like them. Jazz thought they represented her best work. Two of the canvases might have been classified impressionistic — trees with and without leaves. The fifth was a self-portrait, dark and foreboding. "I guess this is it, Kendra. What do you think?"

"They don't have very much colors," Kendra said. She wrinkled her nose at Jazz, as if she were afraid she'd hurt Jazz's feelings. "I like the shapes though!"

"Well, you're right about not much color," Jazz admitted. Lately, she'd been fascinated with light and dark, shadows and shades. Jazz was usually her own toughest critic, but she liked the combination of these paintings as a whole. They formed a kind of study in light and dark.

"Mrs. Gilly at our school paints pretty pictures. Happy pictures. I love red and orange. Don't you?" Kendra asked.

"Mmm-hmm." Jazz squinted at the painting in the center then moved it next to the self-portrait.

"And Mrs. Gilly says we should use lots and lots of colors in our pictures. That's what I learned."

"What? Yeah. I'm sure Mrs. Gilly is a good teacher." Jazz could use all of these in the exhibit, she decided. She just needed a couple of touches on *Trees*. She shook her head, still trying to grasp what this could mean to her art career. Jazz spun around to Kendra. "Kendra, this is my big break, the one I've been waiting for. Do you know what I'm talking about?"

Kendra nodded, wide-eyed. "It's important."

"Really important. I want people to love my painting."

Kendra turned and pointed at Jazz's portrait of herself. "Who's that?"

Jazz grinned. "That's me."

Kendra frowned at the painting then frowned back at Jazz. "You look sad."

Jazz couldn't stand it. She had to tell her friends. There was no way she could wait for the blog meeting. "Kendra, will you be okay until Mom gets back? I need to go talk to Gracie and Storm at the supermarket. Okay?"

"Okay."

Big Lake Foods wasn't far off, just across the highway and a little west. Grace Doe, founder and chief blogger for *That's What You Think!* usually worked as a bagger on Saturdays. So did Storm Novelo, whose job on the website was to write a trivia blog. Today they both had early shifts at Big Lake Foods, which was why the blog meeting had been bumped to noon.

Jazz stopped outside the grocery store. She glanced around for a piece of paper and ended up finding a relatively clean piece in the trashcan. Then she sketched a cartoon of a skinny man telling a young black woman, "You can have your own art show." With that, she dashed inside.

Gracie was a stickler when it came to her job. So Jazz grabbed a box of animal crackers before stepping into Gracie's checkout lane.

"Hey, Jazz! What are you doing here?" Gracie glanced up, but kept bagging.

The cashier rang up the crackers. "Cash or charge?" She reached back and shoved in one of the hundreds of bobby pins that held her bright red hair in a beehive shape on top of her head.

Jazz handed her a five. "Cash, thanks."

"Paper or plastic?" Gracie asked, dangling the animal cracker box by its string.

"Funny," Jazz said. "I just came through so I could give you this." Jazz handed Gracie the cartoon she'd drawn outside.

"Jazz, you could have waited until the meeting." Gracie started to put the cartoon into her pocket.

"You have to look at it now," Jazz ordered.

"I'm busy, Jazz."

Jazz glanced behind her. No line. "Now, Gracie."

Gracie unfolded the crumpled piece of paper and frowned at the cartoon. "I don't get it."

"He's telling her she can have her own art exhibition," Jazz explained.

"And . . . ?" Gracie raised her eyebrows at Jazz.

Jazz felt her smile break through.

Then Gracie's did too. "Jazz! Are you telling me you're getting your own art exhibition?"

Jazz nodded. "At Farley's. Next Friday night. He'll show some of his prints from New York, but I'm the only artist he's featuring. He wants half a dozen paintings."

The usually reserved Grace Doe looked as excited as Jazz had ever seen her. "Man! Way cool, Jazz. That is so tight! Congratulations."

"What's going on over there?" Storm shouted. She was bagging groceries in the checkout behind Gracie's. The line at Storm's counter stretched into the aisle.

"Thanks, Gracie," Jazz said, making her way over to Storm.

"We'll celebrate this afternoon!" Gracie called after her.

"Celebrate what?" Storm demanded.

Jazz didn't bother with the cartoon for Storm. She told her straight out about the art show then stood back.

"Wah-hoo!" Storm screamed. "Sweet! You rock, Jazz Fletcher!" Storm stopped bagging groceries and leaped up onto the checkout counter. "Hey, everybody!" She put her two index fingers in her mouth and let out a piercing whistle. Storm was wearing a red and orange striped blouse with pink stretch pants. She grabbed the intercom mike and made her announcement: "Listen up! My friend here, Jasmine Fletcher, is going to have her own one-woman art show! So you better be there! Farley's Frames!" She bent down to Jazz. "When is it?"

"Friday night, seven to nine," Jazz replied.

Storm repeated the information at full volume, then hopped back down to earth.

As Jazz left the store, a dozen customers congratulated her.

She'd have just enough time to take another look at her paintings before heading over for the blog meeting. Jazz breathed in the scent of potted flowers in front of the store. The sky looked bluer than it had in months as she crossed the highway toward home.

Her mom's car sat in the driveway. Jazz hurried in to tell her the good news.

She found her mother in the living room, deep in a phone conversation.

"I understand that," Mom was saying in her stockbroker voice. "What I don't think *you* understand is the fluctuation percentage." She lifted her chin when Jazz approached, then raised her finger. The "wait until I'm finished" sign.

Jazz turned and walked up to her room. Hard to tell how long her mother might take when she was yelling at someone. She'd tell her parents later. She didn't want anything to bring her down now.

The door to her art studio was partly open, and the light on. Jazz couldn't remember leaving the light on. She pushed open the door and started toward her paintings.

She stopped.

Everything stopped. The air went out of the room.

This couldn't be happening.

Her paintings. Each one had been painted over. Bright red circles covered her impressionistic trees. The canvas next to it had an upturned red line, like a faceless, bloody smile. The rest of the paintings had splatters of red all over them. Her entire self-portrait had been scribbled over.

"Do you like it?" Kendra had come in behind her. She walked up to the canvases, red paint dripping from her paintbrush like thick drops of blood. "I gave you pretty hair on that one. And I made those paintings happy!"

Jazz wheeled around on her sister. Her throat burned with tears and swallowed screams. Her heart pounded in her ears. "How could you?" she cried. "You've ruined everything!"

3

Kendra's smile melted like candle wax. "You don't like it better?" She squinted at Jazz's self-portrait, like she was trying to see into the face of the painting. All the while, Kendra clutched the blood-red paintbrush in her fist as if it were a knife. Jazz watched as her sister raised the brush, dripping globs of red, and brought it down on the painting.

Jazz lunged at Kendra and grabbed the brush out of her hand. Red paint splattered everywhere — on the wall, the floor, the ceiling. On Kendra.

"But... you... you said you like red." Kendra's words dripped out between breathy sobs.

"How could you do this?" Jazz's head was spinning out of control.

Kendra shouted, but her words came in spurts. "I just wanted... teacher said colors... to make them happy!"

The ugly canvas blurred as Jazz stared at it. The portrait was hideous, laughing at her. One minute ago Jazz had been the happiest she'd ever been in her whole life. And now? Now her dream was gone. Over. She wanted to throw something. Kick something. "Get out of my room!" she screamed. She wanted Kendra out. Out of her room. Out of her reach. Out of her sight. "Now!"

"Jasmine! What is wrong with you?" Her mother shouted from the doorway. Kendra ran to her mother's arms. "What did you say to her? Jasmine? What did you do?"

What did I do? This was so typical of her mother. Everything was Jasmine's fault. Jazz's chest heaved with a rage she'd never known possible. She charged toward them. Holding them with her glare, she grabbed her door and shut it. Hard.

"Jasmine!" her mother shouted from the other side of the door.

Jazz spun around and leaned back on her door. "Leave me alone!" She lowered her voice. It took everything she had. "Please. Just leave me alone." She stayed there, her back against the door, listening to Kendra's sobs, to her mother's unanswered questions.

Finally, she heard their footsteps move off down the hall. Their voices grew fainter until they disappeared. Jazz crumpled to the floor and cried silently, the only sound escaping an occasional gasp of air.

When she was out of tears, spent and exhausted, she got to her feet. She had to get out of there. No way could she even look at the paintings. Or see Kendra. Or talk to her mother. She glanced at the clock. Ten past twelve. She might as well go to the blog meeting and take back her big announcement before it spread any further. She sure couldn't stay in this room any longer.

Jazz stepped into the hallway and looked both ways before taking the stairs and stealing out of the house.

On the walk to the cottage, where the blog team met to plot out their website and blogs, Jazz tried to get hold of her emotions. She needed to control herself. Kendra didn't know any better. She was trying to help. All she meant to do was to brighten the paintings like her teacher had taught her to.

Yet no matter what Jazz tried to tell herself, she couldn't make her heart stop pounding or her breathing level out. Anger continued bubbling inside of her, threatening to boil over.

She glanced to the trees and sky, but their Creator seemed far away, too distant from this earthly mess to do anything to help the way she felt. How could God, way off in heaven, begin to understand what she was going through? Jazz picked up a rock and flung it as hard as she could against a tree.

That didn't help either.

She couldn't remember a time when she hadn't felt anger lurking beneath the surface of her skin. Sometimes she thought she'd inherited her anger. Jazz's parents never talked about DC, the brother Jazz never knew. She'd been a baby when DC was killed in a drive-by shooting. Her parents had gone back to school and worked hard to get their family out of Cleveland and into a better life. They'd left the inner city far behind them, but not the anger.

Jazz tried to think of times when she'd felt totally happy — like the day her dad picked her artwork to display in his office building, or the time Kendra won a bronze medal in Special Olympics swimming. Yet even then, anger was never far away. It hung around like a shadow, even in sunshine. And there didn't seem to be much she could do to keep it from surfacing or even exploding.

When she closed her eyes, the hideous self-portrait leaped into her mind. And with it came a searing anger. Jazz didn't want to be mad at her sister, but the anger was there in spite of any rationalizing she could do. And that made it worse. She was still angry at Kendra. But now she was angry at the anger.

When she got to the highway, Jazz raced across, darting between cars. Someone honked at her. She turned to shake her fist at the speeding red sports car. Her foot squished into something as she neared the curb. She caught her balance and looked down to see what she'd stepped in. Dog doo-doo. Of course! What else? She stood by the curb and dragged her foot in the grass, trying to get the gunk off her white tennis shoes. Instead, she just added green grass stain.

Jazz lost it. She wheeled back and kicked the curb.

"Yeow!" Her whole foot throbbed. She hopped on one foot, then dropped to the ground and tore off her shoe. Her hand came away, brown from dog doo. Her foot felt like nails were being hammered through her flesh and bone.

Slowly, Jazz pulled off her sock. Two toes were bright red. Her big toe was already starting to swell. Under the toenail the skin looked purple. She wiggled her toes. They wiggled okay. But her big toe pounded with pain.

Jazz got to her feet. It wasn't that far to the cottage. Taking her time, one shoe on, one shoe off, she hobbled the rest of the way. All she wanted to do was wash her hands, wash her foot, wash her shoe, and hold her head underwater until she woke up from this nightmare.

Annie's car was in the driveway, parked crooked as always. The door to Gracie's mom's cottage was partly open, so Jazz limped on in.

"Surprise!" A medley of voices rang out as the whole blog team rushed up to congratulate her.

As they got closer, their cheers faded into a stunned silence.

"What happened?" Annie asked. Before Annie became Professor Love on their website, her blog name had been Bouncy Perky Girl. Now, all the bounce drained out of her. "You look terrible!"

"I suppose you have an excuse for being so late," Gracie said, eyeing her up and down.

"Don't take this the wrong way," Storm began. "But you stink."

"How could I possibly take that the wrong way?" Jazz asked. She was beginning to wish she'd never come. What was she thinking? They'd want to know why she looked like this. They'd want to know about the art show. The art show that was no more. She didn't want to talk about it.

Mick was the first one to offer any real help. "Come on into the bathroom, Jazz." She took the smelly shoe from Jazz's clutches and led her to the gilded gold and white tiled bathroom. "Your toe looks like you really hurt it." Mick ran water in the tub and passed Jazz a soapy washcloth for her face and hands. "Soak your feet. I'll go put your shoes in the washer."

Jazz could only nod and mutter thanks. Mick was the youngest member of the blog team, but Jazz thought that, in ways, Mick was the most grown-up person she knew. It felt good to sink her feet into the warm water. Closing her eyes, Jazz willed herself to relax. Inhale, exhale. This was nobody's fault. It didn't do any good to get angry. Anger didn't change things.

Jazz opened her eyes. This was *so* not working.

"What's with you, Jazz?" Annie walked in and peered around Jazz into the tub. "Blisters? I get them all the time. All of my shoes are too tight, but I can't stand the embarrassment of buying shoes in my real size." She leaned over to get a better look. "Your feet aren't big at all."

Jazz wasn't always sure how to respond to Annie. Before joining the blog team, Jazz never would have believed that she and Annie Lind would end up friends. Annie was so... so... bouncy and perky, a born cheerleader, with a smile for everybody. If Annie painted a self-portrait, it would have been bright and colorful, the exact opposite of Jazz's. And yet, somehow, they'd become friends. Good friends.

Annie was still staring at Jazz's soaking feet. "No. I'll bet you're no more than a size seven." She sighed. "I would kill to fit into a size seven open-toed pump. But I haven't seen seven since I was... seven."

"They're just feet, Annie." *Sore feet,* Jazz thought.

"Easy for you to say. Anyway, we can't let feet spoil your party! Did you see the sign Mick made?"

Jazz had barely glimpsed the sign as she'd limped in. *Congratulations on the art show!* "That was nice of her. And you. Unfortunately, there's not — "

"You going to stay in here all day?" Gracie asked from the doorway.

"I'm thinking about it," Jazz replied.

Storm scooched into the room in front of Gracie. Mick came in behind her, pretty much filling up the bathroom. "For a woman who's just gotten her own art show," Storm said, "you are totally lacking in grooviness."

"Yeah?" Jazz hated delivering the bad news almost as much as she hated having the bad news to deliver. "Well, maybe that's because there's not going to be an art show."

4

"What do you mean there's not going to be an art show? You couldn't have blown your big chance already!" Storm exclaimed. "You just got it this morning!"

"*I* didn't blow it," Jazz said.

"I'm not getting this," Annie whined.

Jazz pulled her feet out of the tub, stood up, and faced her friends. "There will be no one-woman art show for Jazz Fletcher, thanks to Kendra Fletcher."

"Kendra?" Mick and Annie said it at the same time. Kendra was everybody's favorite, especially Annie's and Mick's. Annie cheered at Kendra's Special Olympics swim meets, and Mick gave Kendra a free ice-cream cone every time she walked into the sandwich shop, where Mick helped out.

Jazz wiped her feet with the towel Mick handed her. "Yep. Kendra."

"Why Kendra?" Storm asked. "Just spit it out, Jazz."

Jazz started to explain, but she saw that Mick was on the verge of tears.

"Is something wrong with Kendra?" Mick asked. "Is she sick?"

"No," Jazz answered. "She's fine. She's even become an artist herself."

"Okay. Now I'm really not getting this," Annie said.

Jazz's stomach tightened. Anger pounded in her chest. It throbbed in her sore toe. It stabbed at the headache that was growing behind her eyes. "My little sister decided my paintings were too gloomy and dark, so she painted over them with red smiley faces. She painted hair and a smile on my self-portrait."

Annie actually laughed. She covered her mouth and tried to turn it into a cough, but it was still a laugh. "I'm sorry, Jazz."

Jazz couldn't believe it. If there'd been anyplace she'd hoped to get some sympathy, some understanding, this was it. "You think this is funny?"

Annie's smile disappeared. "No! It's horrible! You deserve your own art show, Jazz. You do!" She paused. The smile worked its way back into her big blue eyes. "It's just that I can picture sweet Kendra giving you a big smile." She turned her back on Jazz and pretended to cough.

Once again, Mick came to the rescue. "Let's go to the living room and figure out what we can do." She took Jazz by the arm and led her past Annie, Storm, and Gracie. Jazz's toe felt like a log. She walked on her heel.

"Take the couch, Jazz. I'll get you something to drink. Okay?" Mick disappeared into the kitchen, and the others settled in the living room.

Sunlight sliced into colors as it passed through the crystal vase on the coffee table. Even now, even this depressed, Jazz felt like painting it, capturing the interplay of the colors. But what was the use?

"It's a cosmic tragedy," Storm said, sitting cross-legged on the thick white carpet and leaning against the easy chair

Gracie had claimed. "Didn't you try to wipe it off? You know, erase Kendra's bling?"

"You can't just wipe off paint," Jazz explained. Although now that she thought about it, she should have at least tried. But again, what was the use?

"Hey!" Annie cried. "How about fingernail polish remover? That stuff can get rid of anything!"

"If it worked on Kendra's paint, it would wreck my paint too," Jazz said.

They were quiet for a minute.

"Don't you have some other paintings that would work?" Gracie asked. "How about the one you did of your family's voices? I loved that one."

It was one of the pictures Jazz had destroyed in her stupid fit of anger. She didn't want to get into it with Gracie. She shook her head. "I don't have it anymore. I don't have anything except the paintings Kendra wrecked."

"Do overs," Storm said simply. "If you painted it once, you can do it again, right? Do it over."

It was all Jazz could do not to explode in Storm's face. *Do overs?* Could she really believe it was that simple? "You can't recreate art," Jazz explained. "Especially not in a week."

For the next five minutes Jazz dug her fingernails into the heels of her hands as her friends tried to come up with solutions. Each idea was lamer than the last.

"Maybe you could use Kendra's drawings to make an all-new masterpiece!" Mick suggested.

"Far out!" Storm agreed. "Layers of paintings! Like layers of cities archaeologists dig up where my grandparents live in Mexico."

"Or," Annie suggested, "you could turn your paintings into those abstract ones you like to do! Nobody would know the difference."

"I can't believe you don't have more pictures stashed in that mansion of yours," Gracie said.

They took turns coming up with ideas that would only work on a rerun of *I Love Lucy*.

Jazz couldn't take it anymore. "You guys just don't understand!" She hadn't meant to shout. It was like things inside of her were exploding. She got control of her voice and said softer, "I'm sorry, but you don't."

Finally, Gracie got out her trusty notebook. "Well, I'm as sympathetic as the next guy." She turned to Jazz. "We feel for you. If there's anything we can do, let us know. But right now we have to get down to blog business. Okay?"

"Fine," Jazz managed. Business as usual. Gracie was unbelievable. Predictable, but unbelievable.

Gracie pushed ahead, reading some of the comments posted on *That's What You Think!* But Annie took over when Gracie got to Annie's part of the blog, her "Professor Love" column.

"Did you guys see the e-mails I turned in to Mick last night?" Annie asked, springing up and bouncing over to the computer. "Did you post them yet, Mick?"

"Yeah. I did it last night. They were great, Annie."

"Let's see!" Storm joined them at the computer, leaving Jazz and Gracie by themselves.

Jazz couldn't care less about "Professor Love" at this point.

Gracie fidgeted, obviously displeased to have lost control of the blog meeting. "Couldn't we check the site after the meeting?" she pleaded.

"This'll just take a sec," Storm promised. She glanced over at Gracie and Jazz. "Well, if you're too lazy to come over here yourselves, I'll be nice and read it to you." Storm read from the computer screen with the fake accent of an English professor: "'Dear Professor Love; Lately, everything has been getting to me. Even my girlfriend can get me so wound up and angry — over the smallest thing. Like she's started eating candy. Constantly. She's not fat or anything, and most of the candy is sugar free. Still, I watch and listen to her eating and picture her growing into a big piñata, and all I want to do is get a baseball bat, if you know what I mean. (Don't worry. I never would. I'm not the violent type.) Sometimes she wears this stupid mood ring, and all she wants to do is show me how it's changed colors. Drives me postal, I'm telling you! So far, she doesn't have a clue how wound up she makes me. I'm pretty good at keeping my anger bottled up. What else can I do?'"

Storm looked up from the screen. "And it's signed 'Fury.' Let me read Annie's, I mean Professor Love's, answer."

Storm cleared her throat and read: "'Dear Fury; Well, first of all, don't try on that mood ring. If you wear it, I'm afraid it might die of frustration. Second, way to keep that anger bottled up, Fury! Never can tell when a bottle of anger will come in handy. I'm kidding. But obviously, this is no laughing matter. Something's wrong. You can't just pretend it's not. Find someone you can talk to — a parent, your pastor, a school counselor. I don't usually ask where readers stand with God and Jesus. But I do know that if you have a relationship with Christ, he's always there for you to talk things through. Try it! Love, Professor Love.'"

"That was great, Annie!" Mick said, even though she must have read it already when she was posting it.

"You are so kickin', Prof!" Storm said. "There's another e-mail after that one. Let me read — "

"No! That's good," Gracie interrupted. "Great answer, Annie. And I'm sure the next one is just as tight. But I'm doing two shifts at the supermarket today. And I need to get home and finish some homework before I have to head back. Could we stick with planning next week's blog? Please?"

Everybody gathered back by the couch in front of the dormant fireplace. Jazz thought about cutting out, but she wasn't looking forward to the walk back home, not with her toe turning blacker and bluer by the minute.

While Gracie harassed Storm for turning in her trivia column late, Mick whispered to Jazz, "You're not still mad at Kendra, are you?" Mick's sad brown eyes locked on Jazz, and Jazz couldn't imagine Mick ever being mad at anybody.

"No. Of course not. I know she didn't mean to ruin things." But inside, Jazz couldn't keep from finishing her thought. Kendra hadn't meant to ruin everything, but she had.

Mick looked relieved. "Kendra's got to be the sweetest person I know. Since she's been coming to church with us, I've gotten to know her better. I love the way she totally believes and trusts Jesus. She's — "

"Mick?" Gracie frowned at her stepsister. "What's going on?"

Mick grinned back at Gracie. "I was about to tell Jazz that Kendra has a part in the Easter pageant."

"Far out!" Storm exclaimed.

"She's so adorable!" Annie chimed in. "She's one of the weeping women of Jerusalem. Mom gave her a line to say, and she's already got it memorized."

Jazz had overheard Ty teaching the line to Kendra. Over and over. The line was, "They can't do this to Jesus!" For days, every time Ty and Kendra saw each other, they'd both shout, "They can't do this to Jesus!" Jazz was glad her sister got to be in a play, but she'd grown to hate that line.

"Which leads us to the theme of this week's blog," Gracie said, twisting them back on topic. "Since it's Easter week, Mick and I were hoping to have an Easter theme."

Mick sat up straighter. "I'd post a different verse every day, something that fits with Easter."

"And I'll blog on that every day," Gracie added. She turned to Jazz. "Unless anyone has a problem with this."

"I think it rocks!" Storm exclaimed. Storm had become a Christian not too long ago, and she loved everything God and Bible. "I know tons of trivia about Easter. Not just the fact that bunnies don't lay eggs either."

Gracie was still staring at Jazz. Jazz knew the "unless anyone has a problem with this" comment had been directed at her. Who else would complain?

Not Annie. "Sweet!" Annie declared. "Not sure how I'll pull off an Easter 'Professor Love' column, but I'll come up with something."

Now they all turned to Jazz. She didn't care what they blogged on. But having them all stare at her like she was this outsider made her angry. She stood up from the couch and had to grab the couch arm to steady herself. "Whatever you guys want to do is fine with me."

"You sure?" Mick asked.

"Positive. Could I have my shoes back, please?"

Mick dashed to the laundry room and came back with the sneakers. "There. And don't even think about taking my shift at Sam's tonight."

Jazz had forgotten all about taking Mick's shift at the ice-cream shop. Mick and Annie had been trying to get to some Saturday night flea market to find a specific antique doll for Annie's mom's birthday. But one or the other of them, if not both, had to work at Sam's Sammich Shop on Saturday nights. Jazz was supposed to take the shift so they could make it to the flea market. Only last week she'd backed out because of too much homework. And the week before, something else had come up.

"Man, I'm sorry, Mick." Jazz glanced at Annie. "Are you still trying to find that doll for your mom?"

"It's a Charlie McCarthy doll," Annie explained. "Mom had one when she was a kid."

"Somebody said they saw one at that flea market," Mick added. "But we'll get there. Don't worry, Jazz. You take care of your toe."

"It really does look awful," Annie said. "You better let me give you a ride home. I've got the car."

As much as Jazz wanted to be alone, she couldn't bring herself to turn down the offer of a ride. She thanked Mick for cleaning her shoes, then hopped out to Annie's car.

Annie talked the whole drive from the cottage to Jazz's house. Jazz listened as Annie babbled on about the hot new junior who had just moved to Big Lake. She'd met him at Sam's and had accidentally dropped chocolate ice cream on him.

Jazz managed to make the appropriate listening noises: *ah... uh-huh... cool.* But as she watched out her window and took in the same sights that had made her feel close to God on her walk earlier, Jazz couldn't get those peaceful feelings back. Nature wasn't working for her. Not now. Instead, as she smiled at Annie and pretended nothing was wrong, cold flames of anger licked at her heart.

5

Annie pulled her old beater into the driveway behind the new Volvo Jazz's mother had bought herself for her birthday.

"Thanks for the ride," Jazz said, getting out. "Sorry I can't take over at the shop for you guys tonight."

"We'll work it out," Annie said, not sounding mad.

Still, Jazz figured she and Mick had to be at least a little mad. It was the third time in a row she'd backed out on them.

Annie called after her, "Jazz, you sure you're okay?"

Without turning around, Jazz lifted her hand in a half-hearted wave and limped on in.

The last thing Jazz wanted was for her mother to see her like this, so she scurried up the stairs to her room. But the door to the art room was open. Her first thought was that Kendra had come back to finish what she'd started. She flung open the door.

Instead of Kendra, Jazz's dad and brother were there, leaning over her ruined paintings. Jazz wanted to shove them away.

"You're back," Ty said. "What happened to your feet?

"What are you doing?" Jazz snapped.

Her dad turned around to face her. He was wearing dress pants and a white shirt with the sleeves rolled up. She saw him eye her dirty feet, but he didn't ask. "I finished things at the office and got home earlier than I expected. Ty filled me in on what's been going on around here." He arched his back, like it needed the kinks stretched out.

"I was with Mick when Gracie told her about your art show," Ty explained. "I ran home to congratulate you, but you'd already left. Kendra wouldn't tell me what went on, but I kind of figured it out."

"So what are you doing?" Jazz repeated, trying to take the edge out of her voice.

"I told Mom and Dad about your art show thing, and Dad had this great idea," Ty said. "You know how Spiels has that chemical division?"

Jazz didn't know. She knew her dad worked for a big corporation called Spiels, but she had no idea what they did there.

Ty kept babbling. "Dad called and asked them what to use to remove fresh acrylics. They had him read off the ingredients to the chemist guys. You know... from the paints Kendra used. And in, like, twenty minutes this guy shows up at the door with a magic formula! A special paint remover."

"I wouldn't call it magic," Dad corrected. "It's pretty rough going trying to remove the red."

"You've been trying to remove paint from the canvases?" Jazz didn't know what to say. She and her dad hadn't always gotten along. They didn't fight like she and her mom did. But still, you couldn't call them close. They didn't have deep conversations like Annie and her mom did. The subject of art was pretty much avoided by both of them. Jazz knew where her parents stood on that one. They wanted their children to choose safe, practical careers. Being an artist didn't come close to satisfying those requirements.

Yet here he was, trying to salvage her artwork. "I . . . I can't believe . . ."

Dad turned back to the canvas he was working on. "It's not magic," Dad admitted. "And it doesn't seem to work on those three paintings."

"I used acrylics on those and oils on these," Jazz said.

"Ah," Dad said. "That explains it."

"That's probably why everything started coming off when we worked on those three," Ty said.

"Everything started coming off?" Jazz had to fight the urge to grab the rags out of their hands. The three acrylics included the one she'd been working on: *Hot Lunch*. She'd never pull off another *Hot Lunch*.

"These two are coming along nicely, though. Wouldn't you say so, Ty?" Dad stepped back so Jazz could get a better look. The two oils they'd been working on were an abstract-in-progress — although she hadn't worked on it for a while — and her self-portrait. They'd been up on easels, and Kendra had hit them the hardest.

Jazz folded her lips in so words wouldn't come out as she moved in to examine the canvases propped up on easels. The red acrylic Kendra had painted over the oils had started thinning and running down the abstract. That was bad enough. But her self-portrait, with scribbled red hair and a giant, bloody smile looked like something a two-year-old might have painted with finger paints. Jazz had to bite the inside of her cheek to keep from crying.

"Well, they don't look so great now," Ty said quickly, "but see?" He pointed at what had been her cheekbone in the portrait. "I got all the red paint off this part. So we figure the red should come off the whole thing. Right, Dad?"

Jazz turned to the abstract Dad had been working on. It wasn't one of her favorites, and she wouldn't have chosen it for the show. She'd painted part of it with the lights out, while listening to an old CD of Blood, Sweat, and Tears stoked to the max.

Finally, she turned to the three acrylics leaning against her closet. She had to swallow hard to keep herself together. There was no saving *Hot Lunch*. That was clear. The whole concept had depended on separating the smells of the cafeteria, while unifying the whole with color. But now, patches of watery red-gray smeared in spots throughout the composition. Her "grownck" color creation had given in to Kendra's globs of red.

"Your tree paintings were my all-time favorites," Ty said, standing next to her and staring down at the canvases. Kendra's red streaks crisscrossed the paintings. And each canvas had a circular smear, probably where Ty and Dad had tried to clean. "I hate that we ruined those two," Ty said.

"*You* didn't ruin them," Jazz muttered. Even though the two impressionistic tree paintings weren't her favorites, they would have been exactly the kind of art Mr. Farley would have wanted in the show. Now, the only paintings she even had a chance of getting back were her self-portrait, which she couldn't imagine coming clean, the abstract-in-progress Dad had worked on, and the one painting Kendra hadn't gotten to. That one — another abstract meant to suggest sky and hope — was her least favorite of the lot.

Dad glanced at his watch and rubbed the small of his back with his other hand. "I need to take a break, Jasmine. Ty can show you how we've been doing it."

"No problem," Ty said. He took the rag from Dad and refolded it.

"Thanks for trying, Dad," Jazz said, not looking directly at him.

Dad cleared his throat. "Don't thank me yet. I'll check in on you later. Did your mother tell you I have to go out of town for a couple days?"

Jazz shook her head. No surprise. He took these short trips all the time to "make deals."

"I should be back Wednesday night, if everything goes well." He grinned and smoothed his hair, which was still thick and black, graying at the temples. "Maybe all this will be straightened out by the time I get back."

"We'll keep you posted," Ty promised. He turned back to the self-portrait. As soon as Dad left the room, Ty tossed Jazz a rag. "Watch how I do it," he instructed. "Just dip the tip of the rag into this jar." While he talked, he dipped his rag into a glass jar of golden liquid, thin as water. "The trick is to take your time. Just barely dab on the paint you want to get rid of." He touched his rag to a red scribble Kendra had painted for hair. "It won't come up the first time, so you just keep doing little stabs at it like this."

"Thanks for doing this, Ty." She moved to the abstract on the other easel, dipped the rag into the jar, and then tried to rub off a red glob in the center of the abstract.

"Not so hard," Ty warned. He pointed to a red drip spreading from the red glob. "See? That's what happens when you try to rush it. You have to just barely touch it."

They worked in silence, side by side. It was painstaking work. Jazz's head started throbbing about thirty minutes into it. Then her arms tensed. Her toe hurt.

"You're smearing again, Jazz," Ty said.

Jazz threw her rag at the canvas. "This is crazy!" she shouted. "It would take me twenty years to get the paint off this canvas. And I didn't like the painting that much in the first place." She glanced at *Hot Lunch,* smeared and unrecognizable. "*That's* the painting I wanted to show."

"We still have your self-portrait," Ty insisted.

It wasn't enough. She couldn't pull this off. Not by Friday. Jazz sank to the floor. She was glad dusk was falling and Ty couldn't see her face.

"All we can do is try, Jazz," Ty said.

Jazz felt warm tears gathering in the base of her throat, ready to explode out of her.

They were quiet for what seemed like minutes. Then Ty said, "She hasn't come out of her room since you yelled at her."

"I didn't yell at her!" Her defenses shot up automatically. But she *had* yelled at her sister, and she knew it. "Okay. I yelled. But can you blame me?"

He didn't answer. "Mom said you were pretty hard on Kendra."

Jazz's insides twisted. "*I* was hard on *her*?" Ty had no idea what it was like to lose your dream in a split second.

"You know Kendra didn't mean to hurt you. She thought she was helping."

"Don't you think I know that?" She held her head and closed her eyes. White sparks of light fired behind her eyeballs. Her head buzzed. Jazz loved her sister. Sometimes she felt she loved Kendra more than she loved anybody. But she just couldn't handle this. Not now.

"Then you should talk to Kendra and tell her you know she was just trying to help," Ty suggested.

"Back off, Ty," she pleaded.

"Just talk to her, Jazz."

"Ty, please!" she snapped.

"What?" He stopped dabbing and stared at her.

"I need to be by myself and think." She hadn't meant to yell at him. "Listen, I appreciate all you've done here. I do. But I can't handle conversation. Not now. Just let me work on this alone."

Ty put down his rag slowly. "If that's what you want."

What she wanted was to rewind this entire day. Have her paintings back. Start over from the minute Mr. Farley had asked her to show her art.

Ty left the door open a crack, and Jazz got up and closed it. She had to flip the light switch because the room had grown dark. In the bright light, the paintings looked even worse.

She picked up the rag and went back to work on the abstract. Her mind shot her pictures of that morning — finding the door open, seeing Kendra with that dripping paintbrush, the first glimpse of her ruined portrait, and Kendra's face when Jazz screamed at her.

Had Kendra really stayed in her room all afternoon? Didn't she even eat supper? Kendra loved mealtimes.

Jazz knew Ty was right. She should talk to Kendra. But what would she say? Jazz liked being in control. That's why she would never even try beer or alcohol. She didn't want to lose her self-control. It was too important to who she was. Yet lately, she'd felt like she *was* losing control. She didn't want to be this mad at Kendra. She knew the right answers, knew she should talk to her sister and make her feel better.

But she was afraid to. She didn't know what would come out of her mouth. Jazz wasn't at all sure she could control her anger.

Jazz pulled out her iPod and turned up the volume. She'd always been able to disappear into her music, to let it block out her thoughts.

It worked. For a while, at least. For nearly an hour she kept at the dab, dab, dabbing, mindlessly working at red globs, while music filled her head.

But eventually, her thoughts got louder than the music. Even if she cleaned this whole canvas, she still wouldn't have enough for a one-woman art show.

She threw down her rag and yanked off her ear buds. The second the music stopped, there was Kendra in the front of her mind. That face. That sadness.

Ty was right. She had to talk to her sister. She stopped working, cleaned up her work space, then headed for Kendra's room.

Okay, God. It would be nice if you helped me the way you help Mick and the others. This would be a good time to kick in, you know? Jazz hadn't prayed much, even since she'd decided that there was a God. She still believed there was a Creator. She just wasn't sure he could hear her. Or if he heard, she didn't know if he'd do anything about real life. How could he understand it? He was behind everything, but how far behind?

6

Jazz walked down the hall to Kendra's room and knocked on the door. Nobody answered. She knocked harder, and the door creaked open.

Kendra lay in bed, curled up on top of her covers, her face to the wall.

"Kendra?"

Kendra didn't move. Jazz walked closer and peered down at her sister. Kendra's eyes were squeezed shut, the way she used to do when she pretended to be asleep on mornings Jazz woke her for breakfast. She'd wait until Jazz shook her shoulder. Then she'd burst into giggles and shout, "Fooled you!"

Not this time. By the light of the moon streaking through the window, Jazz could see Kendra's soft, fine hair spread over her pillow. The strands on her face were wet with tears.

"I need to talk to you, kiddo," Jazz said. She felt rotten for making Kendra feel like this. "Would you sit up, please, Kendra? I want to tell you I'm sorry." Why hadn't Kendra just stayed in her room that morning, or at least stayed out of Jazz's room? None of this would have happened. As hard as she tried, Jazz couldn't get rid of her anger. She couldn't rationalize it away. The best she could hope to do was hide it from Kendra so the kid wouldn't feel so bad. "Please, honey?"

Kendra sniffed. Then she rolled herself over and scooted up in bed. She wiped her nose with the back of her hand and pushed her hair out of her face. She still wore the pink jogging suit she'd had on earlier, her favorite outfit.

"Have I told you lately how pretty you look in pink?" Jazz tried.

Kendra didn't smile. She just shook her head. Then suddenly, she threw her arms around Jazz and squeezed, hugging her tight. "I'm sorry!" she cried. "I... I didn't mean... *sniff, sniff*... to hurt your pictures." The words came out separated by her sobs. "I wanted... help... make... happy."

Jazz hugged her back. "I know. I know, Kendra. It's okay. I'm sorry I got so mad and yelled. I know you thought you were helping." She waited, holding Kendra in her arms until she felt the sobs slow down and finally stop. "I'm sorry, honey." She held Kendra's shoulders and smiled at her. She loved Kendra's face. The tiny eyes, her big teeth that usually made her smile even bigger. "So we're okay. Right?"

Kendra looked up at Jazz, her forehead wrinkled, her lips pressed together. She shook her head no.

"Honey, you know how much I love you."

Kendra nodded yes.

"So everything's fine. We're fine, right?"

Again, Kendra shook her head no.

"Kendra, please? Don't be mad at me."

Kendra's brow furrowed again. "I'm not mad at you, Jasmine."

"Promise?" Jazz asked, relieved.

"I'm just sad at you."

"Why are you sad, honey?"

"Because you're still mad at me," she answered.

"No, honey. I just lost my temper for a little bit. I'm not mad at you anymore."

"Yes you are." Kendra said it calmly, matter-of-factly.

Jazz shook her head. "I told you I'm not angry at you, Kendra."

"I know you told me. But you are. I can tell."

Jazz started to protest, but she couldn't. As much as she didn't want to be angry with her little sister, she couldn't help herself. "I love you," she said lamely. "And I'm sorry."

"And mad," Kendra said softly. "I have to go to sleep now." She lay down and turned to the wall.

There was nothing to do but get up and walk out. What else could she say? Neither of them wanted it to be true. But it was. Jazz still burned with anger. And she didn't have the slightest idea how to get rid of it.

Jazz slept in and woke to a ringing doorbell. Her head felt foggy, and she wasn't sure what day it was. "Somebody get it!" she shouted. But the bell kept ringing.

"Great," she muttered. She stumbled out of bed and shuffled to the door, slipping on the polished floor. Her toe rammed into her dresser, and she swore. "Can't somebody get the door?"

She hopped to the top step and leaned down to see Kendra and Ty, all dressed up, racing for the door.

Sunday. Her parents would still be sleeping in.

Ty opened the front door. Annie bounced in, and Kendra greeted her with a hug. Annie gazed up the stairs at Jazz. "Hey, Jazz! Don't suppose you want to go to church with us.

Mom's in the car. She's freaking out because I'm making her late."

Jazz yawned. "I'll pass. Have fun. Or whatever."

"See you, Jazz!" Ty waved and dashed out the door.

"Bye, Kendra!" Jazz called down.

Slowly, Kendra turned her head and lifted her face to look up at Jazz. "Bye, Jasmine," she said. But her smile that was always — *always* — there, wasn't.

Jazz toasted a bagel, downed it with milk, and then worked on removing paint from the two oil canvases until Ty and Kendra got home from church. She felt like she had arthritis in her right hand from clutching the stupid, smelly rag. But the original paintings were definitely beginning to surface.

When she heard Kendra and Ty on the stairs, she hurried out to meet them. Finally, Kendra was smiling. "Hey, guys!" Jazz called down. "How was it?"

Before Jazz's eyes, Kendra's huge smile melted. "It was great," she said softly.

"They announced Kendra's Easter play and read her name as one of the actors," Ty said. He glanced at Jazz and gave her a secret shrug when Kendra didn't respond.

"It's so tight that you're going to be in a play, Kendra," Jazz offered. "I've never been in one."

When Kendra still didn't say anything, Ty jumped in. "Mick asked us over to play catch. Better change into jeans, Kendra."

"What about lunch?" Jazz asked.

"Mick said her mom was picking up pizza," Ty said. "You're welcome to come too."

"No thanks. I'm . . . I need to get some things done around here."

"We can save a pizza piece for Jasmine," Kendra told Ty.

Jazz couldn't stand it. As down as Kendra was, she was still looking out for her big sister.

Alone in the house again, Jazz headed for the art room and paint-removal duties. But something made her turn in to her bedroom. She logged onto her computer, suspecting Gracie might have started her Easter blogs already.

Jazz was right. Gracie's first Easter-week blog came up.

• •

THAT'S WHAT YOU THINK!

by Jane

EASTER WEEK

SUBJECT: UNDERSTAND?

Usually I use this blog to share my observations about people and life. This week I decided to do something different. I'm going to try to imagine what I would have observed if I'd lived during the first Easter week. So if you're not into it, well, deal with it. It's my blog.

Can you imagine how great it is in heaven? I don't think we can. Too spun. Too tight for our little brains. So think of your favorite spot on earth. Then multiply it by a hundred zillion and chew on the fact that Jesus left there . . . for here. He left his Father to hang with people like us. He knew they'd make fun of everything he said and that they'd beat him, spit in his face, and nail him to a cross.

Why would he leave heaven for that? Couldn't he have stayed where he was and shouted down to us how we should live our lives?

I'm sure Jesus came down here for a lot of reasons I'm not smart enough to know about. But one reason Jesus came to earth was so we couldn't say he doesn't understand. He does. He went through everything we do, plus a whole lot more. Anybody been flogged? Nailed to a cross? Didn't think so.

And there's an even bigger reason why Jesus came down here. But you'll have to tune in tomorrow to hear that one.

> *For we do not have a high priest who is unable to sympathize with our weaknesses, but we have one who has been tempted in every way, just as we are — yet was without sin.*
>
> —*Hebrews 4:15*

Jazz wondered if Gracie had written this direct hit on her because Jazz had made that crack in the blog meeting about nobody understanding. But she knew Gracie didn't play that way. Jazz knew her friend believed every word she wrote. Gracie believed God understood her. Jazz wondered what that would feel like, to believe somebody always understood.

She went back to her work on the canvases and did her best to tune out everything else. She didn't take breaks, but just kept dabbing and dabbing. After a while, in spite of her innate pessimism, Jazz started to think that the two paintings might actually be okay. The abstract, especially, was coming along. She decided to focus on it, instead of jumping back and forth between the two. She dipped her rag and aimed for her favorite part of the whole painting, the top left corner, where the blues blended into exactly the right color.

Ring Ring Ring Ring Ring Ring!

Her cell blared out "The Star Spangled Banner," the tune Storm had set as a joke on high volume. Startled, Jazz jerked backward. The painting tipped, knocking over her jar of stinky cleaning formula. Jazz lunged for it and grabbed it before it splashed all over the painting. Instead, half the contents sloshed over Jazz.

And still the phone kept ringing.

She grabbed the phone, set down the jar, and stabbed *send*. "What?" she shouted at the phone.

"Whoa!" It was Storm's voice, followed by her unmistakable laugh. "Sorry. I thought I was dialing a friend of mine."

"I just spilled secret formula all over me. I smell like alcohol."

"As much as it pains me," Storm replied, "I'll let that comment pass. Something tells me you're not in a joking mood."

"Did you want something, Storm?" There was no mistaking the impatient edge to her voice, but Jazz couldn't help it. Her cotton Tee stuck to her, and her skin felt clammy. She just hoped there wasn't anything lethal in Spiels' secret formula.

"Um, I think I wanted something, but you kind of scared it out of me."

Jazz took a deep breath. What was it her dad always told her to do when she got angry? Count to eleven. Ten for the anger. One for good measure. Jazz counted to herself as fast as she could. "Okay. I'm sorry. I'm just having a bad day." And counting wasn't helping.

"Sunday?" Storm squealed. "A *bad* day? Surely you jest."

"Not in a jesting mood, Storm. I suppose you're going to tell me I've blown the best day of the week by not going to church?" Mentally, Jazz dared Storm to pull that one, although she had to admit Storm never said things like that. None of her blogging friends did. Even though they hadn't given up inviting her, they never made her feel like a heathen for not taking them up on it.

"I messed up and overslept and didn't even make it to church myself," Storm admitted. "I really like it when I go too. I'm hoping I'll get the hang of going all the time. But I've still had a great Sunday. Did you see Mick's verse on *That's What You Think!*?" She didn't wait for an answer. "It was so tight! I hunted it up in the Bible Gracie gave me and read a whole bunch of pages."

Jazz changed the subject. "And you called because ... ?"

"Oh yeah! Gracie wanted me to call and tell you to call her at home."

"You're kidding."

"Her brother's got her cell for the weekend. Not sure why. But Gracie doesn't know anybody's number unless it's programmed into her cell. Except mine because of all the sevens."

"Why didn't she just — " Jazz stopped. She'd heard enough. "Thanks, Storm. I'll call her."

"Now, Jazz. Sergeant Gracie was very clear about that."

"Now," Jazz promised.

They hung up, and Jazz considered blowing off Gracie and getting back to work. But Gracie would just call her, or get Storm to call her again. Then she'd never get anything done.

She hit Number Five on her cell, then hit *end*, remembering she'd need to call Gracie's house instead of her cell. She had to check her cell phone book to get the home number.

Gracie answered on the second ring. "Jazz?" Obviously, Gracie had a lot of confidence in her commands being followed promptly.

"Hi, Gracie. Storm said you wanted something."

"Yeah. Lisa's brought home enough pizza to feed the football team. Come on over, why don't you?" Lisa was Gracie's stepmom, Mick's mom. Jazz really liked her.

"Thanks, Gracie. Ty told me you guys were doing the pizza thing, but I can't. I'm trying to wipe off Kendra's paint from the only two canvases she didn't destroy totally. Although to be honest, I don't know what difference it will make. Even if I get these cleaned, I still need three more paintings, at least. By Friday. Not going to happen."

"*This* Friday?"

"Told you it was impossible."

"So why won't Mr. Farley put it off a month?"

Jazz fell silent. Not once had she thought about the possibility of buying more time. "Next month?"

"Or longer if you need it. Did you ask him?"

Why hadn't she thought of that? It would solve everything! Jazz could come up with all new paintings. "Gracie, I hate to admit it, but you're a genius!"

"It's a curse," Gracie replied.

7

First thing Monday morning Jazz rolled out of bed and hopped into the shower. She practiced what she could say to convince Mr. Farley to set a later date for her one-woman art show. If he would just give her more time, that would solve everything. She wouldn't even have to worry about cleaning up the two oil canvases. She could create all new artwork.

She pulled her wet hair back and secured it to the top of her head. When she studied herself in the mirror, she looked disturbingly like her mother.

After rifling through her closet, she finally ended up with flared black pants and a white peasant, boho blouse she'd made over Christmas break. The clothes helped. She looked less like her mother and more like an artist. Thankfully, her toe had healed enough so that she could squeeze into her black tennis shoes.

Jazz still had an hour to kill before Farley's Frames opened. She turned on her computer and checked her e-mail. The only nonspam was a message from Storm.

Hey, Jazz!

Thought you could use a little Easter cheer.

Why is a bunny the luckiest creature in the world?
Because it has four rabbit's feet!

What do you call a really smart bunny? An egghead!

Why don't they let bunnies work in the BLHS cafeteria?
Because they refuse to wear a hare net.

Wishing you a day full of grooviness!

—Storm

Jazz glanced at her clock. Still 55 minutes to wait. She logged on to the *That's What You Think!* website and read the second installment of Gracie's Easter blog.

• •

THAT'S WHAT YOU THINK!

by Jane

EASTER WEEK

SUBJECT: THE BIG REASON

What's the big reason why Jesus came to earth? Most of us know the "right answer": He came to die for our sins. But what does that even mean?

I used to want to do everything on my own. If somebody had to die for my sins, I'd die for my own, thank you very much. Not a great idea, when you come to think of it.

I have no trouble believing everybody sins. Especially me. Not just doing things, but thinking things. So okay. Somebody has to pay.

Maybe you're lucky enough to know somebody who might actually die for you. Your mom? Dad? Friend? Maybe. But they can't. They only have one life to offer, and they have to pay for their own sins. So they don't have a life to give you.

What we needed was somebody to live a perfect life and not have his own sin to die for. Then he could die for ours.

He did. That's what Easter's about.

> *Very rarely will anyone die for a righteous man . . . . But God demonstrates his own love for us in this: While we were still sinners, Christ died for us.*
>
> —*Romans 5:7–8*

Jazz read the blog again. The Fletcher family never went to church, except for Ty and Kendra, and even they hadn't been going that long. Still, Jazz knew the whole story about Jesus dying and coming back and all. You couldn't live in America without knowing that. But Gracie had a way of making it sound new — real somehow.

Jazz glanced at the clock again. She had to walk to Farley's Frames, so it was time to get going. Again, she thought through her strategy with Mr. Farley. She didn't want to appear desperate. He'd asked her to bring in more paintings. If she showed up at the store, he'd probably expect her to have something for him. The abstract Kendra hadn't gotten to was the only painting she could offer. It would have to do. She packed it into her portfolio and headed into town.

By the time she reached Main Street, her toe was throbbing again. Gray clouds covered the sky, and it smelled like rain. She walked faster and dashed into the store as the first sprinkles splattered the sidewalk.

Jazz took a deep breath and put on her best smile.

Mr. Farley was with a customer, so Jazz pretended to look around the store. She thumbed through the big craft bins until the customer left. Then she moved to the counter, where Mr. Farley was doing something at the cash register. "Hey, Mr. Farley."

He looked up. "Jasmine, I've been meaning to call you." He glanced at her portfolio and brightened. "Good! You brought me more paintings."

"I just brought one."

"Well, let me see it."

She unwound the string from the circle clasp and pulled out the painting. The light in the store wasn't as good as in her home studio. The blues in the abstract didn't show up as well. She handed it to him.

Mr. Farley frowned at the canvas. "Uh-huh."

She should have known he couldn't appreciate her abstracts. Every print he got in from New York was either classical or impressionistic. Maybe not *every* print, but most of them. She couldn't stand this waiting for him to comment. "So?"

"It's pretty abstract," he observed.

Duh. "I know that's not your favorite style." They'd had this discussion half a dozen times before. "But a lot of people love abstract art." It was taking everything she had not to get into it. She wanted to tell him what real art was.

"Not so many people around here, I'm afraid." He tried looking at the painting from arm's length, then turning it slightly, as if he were trying to make sense of it.

Jazz wanted to grab the canvas out of his hands. But if she could just hold on, maybe she could get what she'd come for. "Well, if you give me more time, Mr. Farley, I could do something else. Something more traditional."

"More time?" He studied her as if she were one more abstract. "I couldn't do that. Friday night's the open house."

"But if we waited, it could be better!" Jazz insisted. "It wouldn't matter if — "

"We're part of Spring Fling." He picked up a flyer from his counter. "See? Right there."

Jazz skimmed down the list of Big Lake Spring Fling activities. Toward the end of the list, it said, "Open House and Art Show, Farley's Frames."

"They didn't have room to put any more than that on this flyer," Mr. Farley explained. "But I'm having some real nice flyers printed up. Blue ones. And you're featured in nice, bold type, Jasmine."

"But the abstract?" Jazz tried, hoping his dislike of her painting could still change his mind.

"Don't you worry about it. We'll run with this one. Just don't bring any more of them. Okay?"

"But — "

"Just bring in those other paintings soon as you can. I want to frame them myself." The little bell over the door rang, and Mr. Farley walked off to meet his customer.

Jazz wanted to take back her painting and crown him with it. She pictured it — his bald head poking through her canvas. She knew she better get out of there while she still could.

It wasn't until Jazz was outside that she realized what had just happened. Not only had she failed in her attempt to buy more time, but she'd lost one of the three finished paintings she had to her name, the abstract she'd been trying to clean. She'd been wasting her time on it.

Suddenly thunder boomed and the gray clouds spilled buckets of rain. Jazz tried to run home, but her toe hurt. She gave up and walked in pouring rain all the way home.

When she got inside, she kicked off her shoes and headed for the stairs.

"Jasmine, you're dripping all over the carpet!" her mother shrieked.

Just what she needed — another mother encounter. "Not now, Mother," she snapped. "I'm begging you."

"Jasmine? I need to talk to you."

"I thought you didn't want me to drip on the carpet. Let me change first." She started up the stairs to get out of her wet clothes.

"Stop!" shouted her mother. "I want to talk to you right now!"

"What is it?" Jazz shouted back.

"I want to know what you said to your sister."

Jazz turned to stare over the banister at her mother. "Kendra?"

"Unless you have another sister I don't know about."

Nobody could argue like Jazz's mother. "I didn't say anything to her. Except that I was sorry for yelling at her."

"Well, you must have said something else because that girl is still moping around the house like her best friend died."

Why did everything have to be Jazz's fault? There was nothing she could say that her mother would believe. "I'm going to take a shower." She trotted up the stairs two at a time. Her mother shouted something after her, but Jazz couldn't hear her anymore.

Jazz turned on the water as hot as she could stand and let the shower pummel her until her skin wrinkled.

For the rest of the day she dabbed at the self-portrait and tried to block everything else out of her mind, everything except the shadowy portrait of herself lying hidden under streaks of red.

8

Tuesday morning Jazz examined the self-portrait in the light of day. The only other paintings for the art show were her portrait of Storm hanging in the shop and the abstract Mr. Farley hated. Even if she salvaged this self-portrait, where was she going to get more paintings? She gave up and plopped on her bed with her iPod just as the phone rang.

Jazz checked her cell screen and saw it was Storm. She had flashbacks to their last phone conversation. "Hey, Storm. Don't tell me. Gracie wants me to call her again?"

"And good morning to you too, Jazz!" Storm said in a way-too-cheery voice. "Don't be knicked out. All is well. I, Storm Novelo, have come up with a perfect plan to get you in good standing in your one-woman art show."

Jazz sighed deeply into the phone. "I'm listening."

"I know where you can get two fantastic paintings!"

"I'm sure you do, Storm. But they have to be *my* paintings. Understand?"

"I get it. Now, will you pay attention, please? All you have to do is call Ms. B and — "

"Ms. Biederman?" Jazz shouted. Their art teacher, Ms. B hated originality. You had to be a pretty horrible teacher to get Jazz to hate art class, but Ms. B had managed it. In her class, all they did was paint things that could have been better shown in a good photograph. "You want me to share my art show with Ms. B?"

"If you'd let me finish," Storm pleaded, "you'd get it. I'd have to be knicked out to want Ms. B and you — or your paintings — in the same room."

"Exactly!" Jazz exclaimed.

"All right then. So, I want you to call Ms. B and ask her — "

"Why do I have to call her?" Jazz demanded.

Storm growled into the phone. "Jasmine Fletcher, think! Right now in the art room at Big Lake High School, you have at least two great paintings that I know of."

Jazz was confused. "What are you talking about?"

"Don't you remember? Ms. B kept some of your stuff for the open house that never was."

A huge snowstorm had made them cancel the high school's open house. Jazz wracked her brain to remember which paintings of hers were supposed to have been displayed. Almost everything she did for Ms. B was forgettable as far as she was concerned. "One was a landscape," she said, remembering that Ms. B had brought in photos and told them to choose which photo to reproduce.

"Yeah! And yours rocked!"

It hadn't. But Mr. Farley might like it. She'd chosen a winter farm scene, with a barn and fields. A couple of things about it hadn't been that bad actually. She'd even thought about reworking it when she got it home. "I can't remember any of the other paintings. Probably a still life. Do you think she still has them?"

"Of course, she does. Ms. B never throws anything away. You know that. She reuses her lunch sack. Call her and say you need your pictures back."

Two more paintings. Maybe, just maybe... "Storm, this isn't bad."

"So call her!"

"Call Ms. Biederman? She hates me."

"True," Storm agreed. "Call her anyway."

Jazz supposed that Ms. B didn't really hate *her*, just her cutting-edge art. Still, Jazz had never pictured their art teacher as having a home outside the art room. "Do you know her number?"

"She's on my speed dial — not! Got a phone book? Or Internet white pages?"

"I'll do it."

"Call me!"

Jazz had left her computer on. All she had to do was go to White Pages and type in Biederman, Big Lake, Ohio. "Figured you were one of a kind," she muttered when only one name popped up: Flower Biederman. Jazz could hardly wait to tell Storm and Gracie that their art teacher's name was Flower. It conjured up images of "flower children," hippies from the sixties, instead of the real Ms. B, who'd probably been born in a three-piece business suit.

Jazz tried to figure out what she'd say. Finally, she just gave up and dialed the number.

It rang. And rang. And rang. After eight rings, the answering machine picked up and a male robotic voice repeated the number and invited her to leave a message.

Jazz hung up and dialed Storm. When Storm picked up, Jazz got right to the point. "I called the number listed for Ms. B in the white pages and nobody answered."

"May I ask who's calling, please?" Storm asked.

Jazz ignored her. "It was that robot message that comes with an answering machine. She didn't even bother to record her own message. What are we supposed to do now?"

"Hmm.... Try again?"

Jazz realized she was squeezing her cell so hard that her hand was shaking. She didn't know if she was mad at Ms. B for not being home, or at Storm for...for being Storm. "I'll keep calling her. But you better be coming up with a Plan B, because I can't just wait for Ms. B to come back from wherever she is."

Jazz tried Ms. B's number all afternoon. Through the evening, she kept working on removing paint from the self-portrait, stopping periodically to hit redial and wait for Robot Man before she hung up. She heard Annie's mom come to take Kendra to church for play practice, but she stayed in her room. She didn't go out when she heard Kendra return.

At ten o'clock, Jazz made her last call to Ms. Biederman. This time she left a message begging her art teacher to call her the second she received this message. Then she ended the call, threw her cell across the room, and went to bed.

In the morning, Jazz's mother pounded on her bedroom door. "Jasmine! Wake up! Get the phone!"

Jazz couldn't believe she'd slept so long. She reached for the phone beside her bed. "Hello?"

"Jazz, what's wrong with your cell?"

"Storm?"

"I've been calling you all morning, and your cell keeps going right to your voice message."

Jazz looked around for her cell phone. Then she remembered tossing it across the room the night before. Her bedroom phone was a cordless one, so she carried it with her to search for the missing cell. She found it next to the wall, flipped on its side. She tried turning it on, but it wouldn't go. "Guess my cell's broken. What's up, Storm?"

"That's why I'm calling *you*! To find out what's up with Ms. B."

"Nothing. She never answered."

"That's what I was afraid of," Storm admitted.

All the tension, the anger, came rushing back the more awake Jazz got. Nothing was working out. Every pinch of hope got squelched. She felt like screaming. "So tell me, Storm. What am I supposed to do now?"

9

"Call the janitor, of course!" Storm shouted through the phone waves. "We don't need Ms. B to get the paintings back. They're your paintings."

"The janitor?"

"Well, technically, the school maintenance director," Storm said.

"I don't know his name."

Storm gasped. "You don't know your own school janitor's name?"

"I don't know a lot of people's names. Do you know?"

"Are you kidding?" Storm asked. "Name, rank, and serial number. He and I go way back. He's a great guy! They're expecting their first baby! But don't tell anybody because they're keeping it a secret until Estelle is further along. They met in Arizona, of all places, when he and — "

"Storm!" Jazz's patience had run out like sand in a minute glass, instead of an hourglass. "Could we save his life's story for another time?"

"Sure. Call him. He is filled with niceness and helpfulness. He'll let us in. I guarantee it."

"*You* should call him," Jazz said. She wasn't sure what she'd do if he turned her down. But he wouldn't turn Storm down.

"Fasheezy! No prob."

"Sweet! Thanks, Storm. Will you call me back as soon as you talk to him?"

"Deal. In the meantime, you can read my Easter blog. Mick just posted it."

Jazz hung up and logged onto *That's What You Think!* She went straight to Storm's blog:

• • • • • • • • • • •

DIDYANOSE

SUBJECT: EASTER

Ever wonder why you never know what date Easter's going to be? It's pretty tricky!

Did you know that Easter is celebrated on the first Sunday after the first full moon that comes on or after March 21 because that's the Vernal Equinox and the start of spring? (Don't make me say that again!) Eastern Orthodox churches figure in even more factors, so sometimes they end up celebrating Easter later than the rest of us.

There's a reason ham is kind of an Easter tradition for dinner. Before we had freezers and refrigerators, we had to eat meat when it was ready to be eaten. So since hogs were butchered in the fall, then cured for six or seven months, they were good eating on Easter.

I hate to be the one to break it to you, but rabbits don't lay eggs.

Each Easter, over one billion Easter eggs are hidden for Easter egg hunts from backyards to the White House lawn. One billion! Wonder how many are found . . .

Americans spent two billion dollars on Easter candy last year (and that doesn't count dentist bills).

Sixty million chocolate Easter bunnies are sold each year. And where does bunny eating begin? Almost three-fourths of bunny-eating kids start at the ears.

So much for Easter trivia.

Now, think about the opposite of trivia. Vital information? Necessary facts? Super important things everybody should know?

Jesus was born.

He lived a perfect life.

He was nailed to a cross and died.

He came back to life on the first Easter!

Easter is filled with grooviness!

The last part of Storm's blog took Jazz by surprise. Storm hadn't been into Jesus very long. She and Jazz had been the holdouts on the blog team. Sometimes, like when they started talking about Jesus or the Bible, Jazz felt left out. But most of time, the blog team was the one place she felt she really belonged.

A glance at the clock told her she had to get back to work on paint-removal detail. She'd just dipped her rag into the remover when her mother appeared at her door again.

"Jasmine, I don't have to be into the office until after noon. That should give us enough time to check out Dillard's new spring line at Great Northern Mall."

Jazz's radar went up. Since her mother only shopped in New York or at a few exclusive designer shops on the other side of Cleveland, that meant the real purpose of this little mall trek was to outfit Jazz in mother-approved apparel. Jazz preferred to design and make her own clothes. She had her own style, and it definitely did not agree with her mother's tastes.

"Thanks for the offer," Jazz said, "but I just have too much to do here."

"Jasmine, you're on break. You have time to do whatever it is you do. I, however, have virtually no other time I can shop with you."

Jazz and her mother hadn't talked about the art show or Jazz's paintings since Saturday's blowup. Jazz wondered if her mom had forgotten about the possibility of the art show this weekend. Or if she just didn't care. Jazz felt flames of anger surging from her toes and rising through her body. "I understand how busy you are. But *you* have to understand that what I'm doing is important. At least it's important to me."

Her mother's face tightened, and she inhaled deeply before speaking. "I am not going to get into it with you, Jasmine." Jazz started to say something, but Mom cut her off. "Change your clothes. You can't go out in public dressed like that. I'll be waiting downstairs."

Jazz ran to the doorway and said to her mother's back, "I'm expecting a phone call!"

Without turning around, Mom replied, "You can bring your cell along."

"It's broken," Jazz tried.

That made her mother stop. But she still didn't turn around. "One more reason to visit the mall. We'll get you a new phone."

Shopping spree was much too happy a phrase to describe what Jazz and her mother experienced for the next four hours at the mall. They fought over shoes, purses, shirts, pants, dresses, even fingernail polish. In one department, they caused such a scene that the clerk asked them to please keep it down.

They drove home in absolute silence, each fleeing to her side of the house as soon as they walked in. Jazz heard doors slam as she climbed the stairs to her room, where she promptly slammed her own door.

"The Star Spangled Banner" rang as she crossed to the computer. The guy in the phone shop had dumped everything from her old phone onto her new phone, including Storm's patriotic ring setting. Jazz had to dig through bags to answer it. "What?"

"Charming as ever, I see," Storm chirped. "Nobody answered your house phone, so I thought I'd give your broken cell a try, for old time's sake. And here you are!"

"What did he say? Will the janitor let us in the school?" Jazz kicked off her shoes and collapsed onto her bed. Her toe ached. The Japanese food she'd eaten at the mall was getting revenge on her stomach.

"No can do," Storm answered.

"But you said he was your friend! You said he'd do it." Jazz had been counting on this. Right now it seemed like her only chance to pull off the show by Friday.

"And he *would* help," Storm assured her, "if he weren't in the Bahamas."

"The Bahamas?" Some of Jazz's classmates got to go on vacations every spring break. Others couldn't afford it. Then there were still others, like Jazz, whose families could afford a vacation but never went because of work. *Why couldn't my father have been a janitor?* "Then it's over."

"Not necessarily," Storm said.

"If I can't get those two paintings, how can I pull off an art show? I needed them, Storm. Mr. Farley won't change the date."

"We'll get the paintings." Storm sounded so sure. Infuriatingly sure.

"How?"

"You know what they say. 'When one door shuts, look for the open window.' I'll come over and explain in person. Tonight."

"But — "

"Trust me. See ya! Ten-ish." She hung up.

Jazz got so nervous waiting for Storm to show that she planted herself in front of the TV and turned on a reality show. Ty sat and watched about ten minutes of it with her before going to his room to call Mick. Kendra walked through, and Jazz tried to get her to watch something. Anything.

Kendra was sweet and polite, but she shook her head. "No thanks. You're still mad."

Jazz protested. She tried to laugh it off. But Kendra knew what she knew, and Jazz couldn't change either of them.

Finally, Storm arrived. "You need a jacket," she whispered, standing in the doorway.

"You're not coming in? Why do I — ?"

"And a flashlight," Storm whispered again.

"Storm, why are you whispering?"

"I'll wait out here." Storm closed the door.

Jazz slipped on a jacket and found a flashlight. When she came out, Storm was standing all the way down the end of the walk. A cold wind shook the few leaves on the trees. A few stars stretched over rooftops.

Storm motioned for her to hurry up.

"So what's all the secrecy?" Jazz asked, zipping her jacket against the wind. "Where are we going?"

"Big Lake High School." Storm set out at a fast pace. "Remember that saying about one door closing and a window opening somewhere?"

"So?"

"So we're going to find that window and climb in to get your paintings."

10

Jazz had to jog to keep up with Storm, even though Storm had shorter legs. "Wait a minute!" Jazz shouted. "What do you mean 'climb in' and get my paintings? Storm?"

In the dark, Storm's yellow boots reflected a tiny bit of light from a streetlight as she spun around to face Jazz. "Would you like me to get you a loud speaker so you can alert the whole town to our break-in?"

"Break-in?" Jazz shouted even louder. She stopped in her tracks. "We're breaking into school?" She'd fantasized about breaking *out* of school. But never *in* to school.

Storm locked her arm through Jazz's and marched on toward the high school. "It's not really breaking in," she explained. "Mr. Reed — "

"Who's Mr. Reed?" Jazz interrupted. A dozen possibilities rose to mind. An accomplice? A robber buddy?

"Mr. Reed, the janitor."

"Who's in the Bahamas..."

"Right. Mr. Reed," Storm continued, "says that *we* actually own the school. It's a public school, and we're part of the public. Not to mention that it's our taxes — yours more than mine — that pay for the building."

Storm had a point, but Jazz didn't feel like giving it to her just yet. "Go on, Storm. I want to hear your rationalization on break-ins."

"We won't be breaking in!" Storm insisted. The school was in view now, looming in shadows cast by the lights in the school lot. "There's a window that never quite closes all the way."

"And you know this because ...?"

"Don't worry," Storm said. "This isn't my first nonbreak-in."

"Now I feel much better," Jazz said sarcastically.

"Yeah. I run out of books over the holidays. Did you know that even the public library closes on holidays? Is that out of line or what? I mean, when do you have more time to read than on a holiday? What am I supposed to do when I run out of books?"

"Break into the school library, of course," Jazz said, the light dawning. Storm read all the time. Her room had stacks of books in every corner, most of them checked out from the library.

"Exactly! Mr. Reed knows about the weak window latch, which is in the kitchen, not the library. We agreed he wouldn't fix it, in case of emergencies. Like this one!"

They were only a few yards from the school. Storm crouched and made a dash for a bush next to the building.

Jazz followed. "So if it's not really a break-in," she whispered, shoving a sprig of evergreen out of her face, "why are we sneaking in?"

"Not everyone is as cool as Mr. Reed," Storm explained. She stood up and dashed toward a window. "Besides," she whispered, turning back, "it's much more fun this way!"

Fun? Jazz glanced over her shoulder and ran up to Storm. "This is so *not* fun!"

Storm turned to her, shrugged, and then stood up, totally out in the open, where a streetlight illuminated her shiny black hair. "Okay. We won't play cops and robbers, then. Come with me." She walked like a normal person around the side of the school to the kitchen.

Jazz felt like an idiot.

At the first window, Storm pushed and shoved and pushed again. The window refused to budge. "Hmmm... Maybe it was that window." She moved to the next window, but it was locked too. The third window creaked and then slid straight up. "That's the one!" Storm exclaimed. "Sweet!"

Storm had Jazz boost her up and into the window. Then Jazz managed it on her own.

"Hungry?" Storm asked. They were standing in the middle of the dark, empty kitchen.

"The art room, Storm?" Jazz pleaded.

"Okay. But you don't know what you're missing. Bound to be frozen fish sticks in there. Maybe peas."

"Could we get this over with? Please?" It was creepy being in school with nobody else around.

Their footsteps echoed in the halls as they walked to the art room. Jazz turned on her flashlight to help her get oriented as they traipsed up the hall. "Storm, what if — ?"

" — if the art room's locked?" Storm said, finishing Jazz's question. "No sweat."

But Jazz *was* sweating. When they reached the door to the art room, Jazz grabbed the door handle and pressed.

Nothing. The door was locked. "Now what? We should have known the door would be locked."

"We did know," Storm said, motioning for Jazz to step aside. She reached into the pocket of her balloon pants and pulled out a card.

"What's that?" Jazz asked.

"I don't have a credit card, so I laminated this from my Monopoly game."

"You're going to unlock the door with a Monopoly game card?"

Storm held it up, but Jazz couldn't make it out in the dark. "It's a Get-Out-of-Jail-Free card!" Storm laughed. "Works great for the library." She stuck it in between the door and the door jam, then wiggled and jiggled it.

"Maybe we should just go," Jazz said, getting an uneasy feeling. What if somebody saw them and thought they were breaking in? "The paintings aren't that great. They're not worth going to jail for."

"Don't worry," Storm said, still working the lock. It clicked. Storm waved her card in the air as she opened the door. "We have a Get-Out-of-Jail-Free card!"

Outside light from a streetlight brought the room up to dim. Chairs huddled to one side of the room, half of them upside down on the other half. Jazz sprang into action. "I'll take the closet. You take the art cupboard in the corner."

Jazz vaguely remembered Ms. B storing paintings in the bottom of the coat closet. She shone her flashlight into the closet and searched. She found a box of clay figures, but no paintings.

"There's nothing here!" Storm announced. "I'll check the other cupboard."

Jazz closed the closet, leaving things exactly like she'd found them. At least she hoped they were where she'd found them. Across the room, she heard the cupboard door creak open and the sound of papers being shuffled.

"Jazz!" Storm cried. "I think I've got one! Isn't this yours?"

Jazz ran over the cupboard. Her shin rammed into a chair. "Ow!"

"You okay?" Storm asked. She'd pulled out a painting done on thick construction paper. "I can't see the name on this one, but I think I remember it."

Jazz took the painting and pointed her flashlight at it. "It's mine," she muttered. It was a still life of a vase and flowers. Not very original.

"I love this one!" Storm squealed, her light moving up and down the vase.

"Thanks," Jazz said weakly. Maybe Mr. Farley would like it too. It was definitely traditional, classic. And it was one less painting she had to come up with.

Storm was already ferreting through the deep shelves of the cupboard. "Do you remember what the other painting was, Jazz?"

"A landscape. Like a snowy field and barn with — "

"Got it!" Storm pulled out another painting.

Jazz recognized it instantly. Ms. B had brought in photographs and let them pick which photo they wanted to paint. She and Jazz had gotten into a big argument when Jazz pointed out that it was a waste to paint something exactly like the photograph. Now, Jazz tried to get a good look at her old painting. It wasn't half bad really, if you liked that sort of thing. And Mr. Farley did like that sort of thing.

"Storm, thanks."

"Hey, it was dumb luck finding the paintings."

"No. I mean, thanks for going to all this trouble. I'm not wild about these two paintings, but with these, plus the two Mr. Farley already has, I've got a shot at having enough. If I can get the paint off one more and then maybe come up with something new, I — "

The door to the art room flung open. Storm screamed. Jazz tried to scream, but nothing came out. They grabbed onto each other. A powerful beam of light blinded Jazz as she looked toward the art-room door. She couldn't make out a thing, except the bright white light.

Then a deep voice said, "Freeze! You're under arrest!"

11

Jazz had never been so scared in her whole life. She clung to Storm while her life flashed before her eyes. Not her past, but her future. Her mother would disown her. Jazz would go to jail. She'd beg for pencils to draw on her cell walls.

Storm had been clinging to Jazz as tightly as Jazz had been holding on to her. But now, Storm's grip relaxed. She stepped sideways, leaving the flashlight beam aimed on Jazz. "You really had me going," Storm began.

"I said don't move!" the man shouted.

"Not moving. I'm Storm Novelo, by the way. This is my artistic friend, Jasmine Fletcher."

Great, Jazz thought. She'd been picturing herself "downtown," in the police station, only giving her first name, and that, only after intense interrogation. She was not in a hurry to have the police call in her parents.

"And you are...?" Storm asked, smiling at the holder of the flashlight.

"Officer Bruce Harris."

He lowered his flashlight, and as Jazz's eyes got used to the world again, she could see that he was much younger than she'd thought. He didn't look much older than Gracie, in fact.

Black hair. Some kind of uniform. Maybe security instead of police.

"How did you girls get in here?" Officer Harris held his flashlight like a gun and moved the beam from Storm to Jazz and back again, like he was keeping them covered with it.

"Through the open window," Storm explained, as if it were the most natural thing in the world. "So, like, did somebody call and tattle on us? Rat us out?" She laughed. "I'm really sorry we bothered you, though."

"I'm on duty." He was starting to sound confused.

Jazz wanted out of there. "We weren't doing anything. I mean, anything wrong. I just needed to get my paintings back."

"Your paintings?" He sounded like he didn't believe her.

Storm took over completely then. Beginning with Saturday morning, when Jazz had run into Big Lake Foods bearing the great news about her one-woman art show, Storm led Officer Harris through the tragic accident involving Kendra and red paint, their own feeble attempts to contact Ms. B and Mr. Reed, including a description of the janitor's Bahamas vacation, right up to the present successful hunt for the paintings. Storm talked so fast, it made Jazz's head hurt.

But Storm's words worked their magic on Bruce Harris. He gasped at the account of the ruined paintings, nodded his agreement that Mr. Reed deserved a vacation, and laughed at Storm's description of their break-in.

"Could I see the pictures?" he asked, as if they were standing in an art gallery.

Storm motioned him over for a good look.

"I don't know much about art," he admitted, "but these look really real. I really like the one with all the snow especially."

He and Storm talked a while longer, exchanging stories about being fairly new to Big Lake and how funny it was when they'd discovered there was no big lake. Then he offered to give them a lift.

"A lift home?" Jazz clarified. "So we're not under arrest or anything?"

He chuckled. "No. But let's agree that this will be your last holiday visit to your school, okay?" He turned to Storm. "Maybe you can check out twice as many books just to be safe from now on?"

"Fasheezy," Storm agreed.

Officer Harris dropped off Storm first. But before he did, she filled him full of statistics and trivia about policemen. Jazz was pretty sure that the officer slowed to turtle speed just to have more time to listen to Storm.

"Happy Easter, Officer Harris!" Storm cried, as he pulled up to the curb in front of her house. Storm hopped out and skipped up the sidewalk.

Officer Harris pulled back onto the street and headed for Jazz's. "That girl knows more about the police force than anyone I've ever met. Pretty amazing..."

"You have no idea," Jazz muttered.

It took Jazz a couple of minutes to retrieve her paintings from the back of Officer Harris' cruiser once he'd stopped in front of her house. She tucked the pictures under one arm and shook his hand as they said good-bye on the front lawn.

Suddenly, the front door opened, and Jazz's mother rushed out. Her high heels clicked on the sidewalk. She strutted all the way up to them, then turned to Jazz and said, "Don't say another word."

"But I was only — !" Jazz tried.

Her mother pointed her finger in Jazz's face. "Did you hear me?" she shouted. "Not one word!"

Jazz felt embarrassment mix with anger in a lethal combination.

Officer Harris finally spoke up. "Ma'am, maybe I can clear this up. Your daughter — " But he didn't get a chance to explain.

Jazz's mother turned on him. "If you want to talk to us, you'll have to wait until our lawyer gets here!"

"Mother!" Jazz cried.

Her mother took hold of Jazz's arm and pulled her toward the house.

Officer Harris cleared his throat. "Everything's okay, Mrs... Ma'am. No need for a lawyer."

Jazz craned her neck to look back at Officer Harris. "Thank you!" she shouted, just before her mother slammed the front door.

Her mother glared at her. "Thank you?"

"He was nice!" Jazz insisted.

For the next five minutes, Jazz couldn't get a word in as her mother ranted on about how embarrassing it was to have your daughter brought home in handcuffs. Handcuffs? As if she hadn't noticed that there were no handcuffs and the "police" car read *Security* on the side.

Finally, Jazz got her chance to explain. But it wasn't easy. The "dialogue" quickly sank into a shouting match. Her mother threatened to call Jazz's father, who was still away on business, and tell him what his daughter had been up to while he was away. Jazz threatened to call her father to tell him how Jazz's mother had embarrassed Jazz beyond belief.

She knew if her dad had been home, he could have served as referee. They needed one.

Toward the end of the argument, when Jazz and her mother were both spent, Jazz spotted Ty and Kendra at the top of the stairs. She wondered how much they'd heard. Probably everything. She and her mother weren't exactly whispering.

Jazz hated these fights. She let herself look directly into her mother's eyes. Jazz prayed she'd understand just this once. "I'm sorry. Okay? I just wanted my paintings so I could let Mr. Farley go ahead with my art show."

Her mother gave her a weak attempt at a smile, almost like she wanted peace between them too. Maybe she did. "So now you'll be able to go ahead with your one-woman show?"

"I think so. I might be a painting short. But with these two pictures, I think I may have enough." It was the first time Jazz had let herself think — believe — that things might be okay. Was the art show back on? Was Jazz Fletcher actually going to have her own art show? "Mother, will you come?"

"Of course." She smiled again. "I know we haven't agreed on much lately. But I do know that you have talent, Jazz. I'd like to see your paintings displayed. When's the show?"

Jazz couldn't remember the last time she and her mother had been together like this, with no shouting, no anger seething under the surface. It felt good. "Mr. Farley has flyers for it. My show is from seven to nine Friday night."

Her mother's eyes narrowed. "This Friday?"

Jazz's body stiffened. "Yeah. For the Spring Fling celebra — "

"That's right. I knew there was something. We're having a reception for new members at the country club that evening." She put her hand on Jazz's arm. "I'm sorry, Jasmine. I doubt I'll be able to break away. I'm chair of the welcoming committee. If it were any other time, I — "

Jazz jerked her arm away. "You'd what? Find another excuse?"

"That's not fair, and you know it."

"Fair? You want to talk about *fair*?" Jazz knew she should leave right then. She couldn't think straight. She had no control over what she might say next. "You *never* put my things above your stupid events!"

"Do you hear yourself? You're acting like a two-year-old." Her mother stood and let out a deep breath. "I'm not going to discuss this any further. Especially not tonight."

"Fine," Jazz muttered.

"I'm going to bed, Jasmine. Hopefully, we'll both see things more clearly in the morning. Goodnight."

Jazz thought she could see "things" clearly enough. Instead of attending her own daughter's art show, her mother would be welcoming strangers at the country club.

12

Ty and Kendra weren't on the stairs when Jazz dragged herself up to bed. For an hour she lay in the dark, thrashing, tangling herself in her sheets and blankets, kicking them off, then pulling the covers around her again.

Finally, she gave up on sleep and turned on her computer. She checked her e-mail, then went to *That's What You Think!* and pulled up Gracie's blog.

• •

THAT'S WHAT YOU THINK!

by Jane

EASTER WEEK

SUBJECT: PEACE, MAN!

> *Peace I leave with you; my peace I give you. I do not give to you as the world gives.*
>
> —*John 14:27*

Peace, man!

Yeah, right.

If you're still with me, you know that this week I've been trying to imagine the first Easter week.

Thinking about the Last Supper, I tried to imagine how hard it would have been for Jesus to have a nice meal, knowing what was coming. I mean, he knew how many whip lashes he'd be getting. He knew soldiers would spit in his face and drive nail spikes through his hands and feet. He knew his friends would bail. And still, as he ate that last meal on earth, Jesus tried to make his friends feel better. He promised them they'd get great rooms in heaven, that they'd see him again, and that he'd send his Spirit to help.

And he promised them peace. Peace that was so great they couldn't even understand it. Peace they could never find anywhere else.

What do you do when you're so wound up that you can't have a minute's peace? I've tried lots of things. I've made lists of stuff I had to do: homework, blog, homework, job, homework, chores. I thought that if I could just get everything on that list done, then I could sit back, relax, and have peace. That peace only lasted two minutes. That's how long it took for my mind to fill up with a hundred more items I could put on my to-do list.

I've tried to psych myself into peace: "Jane, nothing is worth worrying about this much. Forget about it. There are people with worse problems than you have. Just don't worry so much. Relax." If you've ever tried this self-talk solution, then you know it's not that great. After all, look who's talking, right? The same person who's been so worried!

Maybe some people have enough money for great Easter vacations on peaceful, sandy shores. But all the money in the world can't buy them inside peace — a calm that's there when you're by yourself or with a mob.

The only lasting peace starts with having peace with God through Jesus. And we can have that because of what he did that first Easter week, dying for our sins and craziness. That's the start of having the kind of peace we won't find anywhere else.

Jazz didn't know whether to laugh or cry. Peace? It was almost as if Gracie had been watching her and seeing the turmoil raging inside of her. Maybe she had? Grace Doe didn't miss much.

Jazz wished she could have that kind of peace. Mick had it. So did Gracie and Annie in their own ways. What would it be like to be a Christian? Jazz wasn't even sure why she put up so much resistance to the idea. Part of it was just a reaction. She didn't want to be like everybody else.

Or did she? Even Storm was different since she'd accepted Christ. Things didn't seem to get to her so much. She was more real too. More herself.

Jazz couldn't stop thinking about it as she climbed back into bed. She wasn't sure what it meant to be a Christian. Was it any different than trying to act more like Christ? She had a feeling Gracie and Mick would have said there was a big difference. But didn't everybody want to be a better person? Maybe all she needed to do was to be nicer and less angry, to do good things, and treat people better. To be a more "Christian" person. It was worth a shot.

In the morning, Jazz woke up determined to be a better person. She took out a writing pad and wrote down the names of people she'd exploded at in the last month. When the list started getting too long, she felt her old frustration turning into mild anger, and she stopped. She crossed off everyone except Ty, blog team, Mother, and Kendra. That would be her start.

Jazz wanted to think of something good, something "Christian," she could do for each person on her list. And she didn't want to wait another day, even though her art show was only thirty-six hours away. She didn't want to put off becoming The New Jazz. Besides, with the two paintings she'd recovered last night, the two Mr. Farley already had, and the self-portrait, she'd have enough for the art show. She thought she'd only need a couple of hours to finish removing the red paint from her self-portrait. She could do that later and still get the paintings to Mr. Farley in time for framing.

Jazz studied her target list. She circled Ty's name. He'd be first because he'd be the easiest. All Ty ever wanted was someone to play ball with.

Jazz found Ty outside, playing catch with Mick.

"Hey, you guys!" Jazz shouted.

They stopped tossing the ball. "Hi, Jazz!" Mick called. "Were we being too loud? Sorry."

"You weren't loud," Jazz said. At first it made her mad that Mick would think that was the only reason she'd joined them. But she brushed the thought aside.

"What's up?" Ty asked. He kept smacking his ball into his glove over and over.

"Nothing," Jazz replied. "I just...you want to play catch?" She felt like a class-A idiot. They were already playing catch.

"Play catch?" Ty repeated. "You mean...with you?"

"Yeah." Jazz tried to look free and easy. "I thought it might be fun."

Nobody said anything for a minute. Then Mick broke the silence. "Sure! I have to go work at Sam's in a little while. But we'd love to have you throw with us."

"You don't have a glove, do you?" Ty asked.

Jazz hadn't thought of that. She shook her head no.

Ty took off his glove and threw it to her. She dropped it. "Thanks, Ty." She picked up Ty's worn leather mitt and pulled it on. It felt small and sweaty.

Jazz was Ty's biggest fan. She went to almost every game when he was playing. But she couldn't remember the last time she'd played catch with him. Or with anyone else, for that matter.

Mick lobbed her the ball, and she managed to catch it. She threw it to Ty, but her throw was way short. He jogged up for the ball and stayed there. They went on like this for what seemed like five hours to Jazz, but was only about five minutes. When she couldn't take the boredom any longer, Jazz said, "Hey! I know you have quit pretty soon, Mick. I'll let you two get back to it. Thanks. It was . . . fun."

"Anytime, Jazz!" Mick called. But Jazz could tell they were glad to get back to real pitching practice.

Doing good things wasn't as easy as she'd hoped.

Jazz waited until Mick had gone into work, then phoned Annie at Sam's Sammich Shop. At least with Annie and Mick, Jazz knew exactly what she should do, what the "Christian" thing to do was. Annie and Mick needed time off.

Annie's mom, Samantha Lind, answered and passed the phone to Annie. "Hey, Jazz! It's been crazy around here! It's like everybody's bored of being home from school, and they've all decided at the same time to come and hang out here. Mom's got both Mick and me waiting tables tonight."

"That's what I wanted to talk to you about, Annie. I know I've backed out of waitressing for you, taking your shift like you wanted. So I'm calling to say I can work for you tonight." Jazz waited. She really did want to do this for Annie. And for Mick. It felt pretty good too.

"Tonight?"

"Yeah. And don't worry about my art show. I'm finishing the last painting this morning and running them over to Farley's. So I'm good for taking the shift, Annie."

"That's so nice of you, Jazz," Annie began. Jazz braced herself for the *but* she could hear was coming. "But that flea market sale only happens on Saturdays."

Jazz had forgotten that. She should wait until Saturday, but she didn't want to. She needed peace now. "But I could do it tonight. In fact, I can do it now."

"Well . . ."

"Annie, I want to do this." Jazz had to fight to control her voice. She struggled to ward off the rising anger that this wasn't going the way she'd imagined it. "I'll work for you guys on Saturday too, okay? But don't I need training?"

"Not really," Annie said.

Jazz saw her opportunity slipping away. She couldn't let it. "Annie, I'm coming over. You said you were busy. And if you guys train me today, you and Mick can take off Saturday night."

Through the phone came Annie's nervous laughter. "Are you okay, Jazz?"

Jazz took a deep breath. "I'll be right there."

She changed clothes three times before settling on an all-black outfit she'd designed last year. Then she jogged most of the way to Sam's Sammich Shop.

Samantha Lind waved her over as soon as Jazz walked into the shop. Beach Boys music played on the jukebox. Annie's mom had decorated the whole place retro, with posters of the Beatles and a beach mural she'd paid Jazz to paint on one wall. Jazz had enjoyed capturing the flavor of those old beach-party movies, but mostly she'd liked the job because of Sam.

"Jasmine Fletcher! Give me a hug." Sam did most of the hugging. "I couldn't believe it when Annie told me you wanted to help out."

Jazz shrugged. "You look pretty busy."

"Lots of people, but little ordering going on."

Annie raced by with a tray of dirty dishes. "You're here! Bet you'll be sorry."

"Annie Lind!" her mother called after her, as Annie hustled to the kitchen with her load of dishes. Sam laughed.

It almost hurt Jazz to watch them together. Annie and her mom were friends. She knew Annie's mom didn't let Annie get away with anything, but you could tell how well they got along, how much they loved each other.

Mick took time out from dipping ice cream and showed Jazz around the kitchen. Then she explained some of the ice-cream dishes and ran through the names of the flavors. Jazz knew most of it because the whole blog team hung out at Sam's.

"So," Mick said when she'd gone over the new menus, "you want the counter or the booths?"

Jazz chose booths. Mick handed her a pad. Annie wished her luck. And Jazz walked to the farthest booth, where three boys, probably around Ty's age, were playing war with their paper straw covers.

"What can I get you?" Jazz asked, clutching her pad and pencil hard.

"Huh?" asked the skinniest boy.

The blond kid laughed. "More straws!"

That cracked up all of them.

"Seriously, what do you want?" Jazz tried again.

"Water." This came from the skinny kid.

"Bottled water?" Jazz started to write it down.

"Duh, no!" the boy replied. "Just in a glass. Regular. With ice."

Jazz tried to be patient. She forced a smile. "Good. What do you want to eat?"

"Fries," said the blond.

Jazz turned to the chubby kid sitting across from the other two. "And you?"

He blew his straw cover at the blond kid. "Some of his fries!"

They were laughing hard as Jazz walked back to the kitchen to put up the order.

When she came back, two older men were settling into a booth. She started over to them, and the blond kid at the next booth leaned out and shouted, "Ketchup! We need ketchup!"

Jazz glanced around until she saw a bottle of ketchup on an empty table. She grabbed it and slammed it down on their table.

"When are my fries coming?" the chubby boy asked.

"They're not your fries, dumbhead!" snapped the blond kid.

Jazz let them fight it out while she took the men's orders. Her stomach churned as the boys in the back booth got louder. When she took them their fries, they already had ketchup spilled on the table.

"These aren't crispy," the chubby kid complained. "I like them crispy."

"They're not yours!" shouted the blond.

They were so obnoxious that they made Jazz mess up her next two orders.

"Hey, you!" yelled the skinny kid.

Jazz clenched her notepad as she trudged to the back booth again. Salt and ketchup covered the table. Granules of salt crunched under her shoes. There wasn't a single fry in sight. Trash littered the ground around the booth.

"I'm not paying for those fries," said the blond. "They weren't crispy."

Jazz gripped the table and stared down each ketchup-smeared face. Then she turned and walked back to the kitchen and found Sam. "Thanks for training me, Sam. See you later."

She didn't wait to tell Annie and Mick good-bye. Jazz hadn't even lasted an hour.

As she walked back home, Jazz hated the way she felt. She'd tried to do the right thing, and it had backfired. She had less peace now than she'd had when she started this quest to be Christian.

13

Back in her room, Jazz took out her list and put a line through "Ty" and "blog team." There were two more names on her list. Maybe those were the two she should have started with. Her mother and her sister. It was where most of her anger had been directed all week.

Jazz had already thought about what she could do for her mother. They hadn't spoken to each other all day. Knowing she couldn't trust herself to say the right things to her mother face-to-face, Jazz decided to do what she did best. She went straight to her art room and got out her supplies.

As she sketched with markers onto the folded construction paper, Jazz remembered making pictures and cards for her parents when she was in elementary school. She'd stopped when it occurred to her that of all the pictures she'd drawn for her mother, not one had ended up on the fridge.

Jazz forced that memory down and worked on the card in front of her. Her mother loved roses — red and yellow roses, no pinks. So that's what Jazz drew. When she finished her drawing, she could almost smell the roses. That's how real they looked. Ms. B would have been proud. And Jazz felt pretty sure that her mother would like them too.

It took a lot longer for Jazz to decide what she should write inside the card. Everything she thought of sounded too sappy. She even tried a poem, but she eventually wadded it up and threw it into the wastebasket with all her other failed attempts. Where was Gracie the Writer when you needed her?

Finally, Jazz settled on a simple, non-rhyming message that said she was sorry for the shouting and the fighting. And she included three coupons, designed by Jazz, of course, and good for any three house chores of her mother's choosing.

If that didn't earn her brownie points with God, Jazz thought, nothing would.

She found her mother sitting at her desk in her den. Jazz had always felt that she needed to knock before entering this room, even when the door was open like it was now. She rapped her knuckles on the door frame.

Her mother looked up from a pile of papers stacked in front of her on the long, wooden desk. She peered over her glasses at Jazz. "Yes?"

Not exactly the greeting Jazz had hoped for, but she pressed on. "Hi. Am I bothering you?" Dumb question. She was obviously disturbing her.

"I'm just paying bills. Is something wrong?"

Jazz felt about five years old as she walked up and handed her mother the card she'd made. Her heart pounded while her mom studied the roses and then opened the card.

Jazz's mother took off her glasses and set them on the desk. "Jasmine, I don't know what to say."

Neither did Jazz.

"Thank you. It's beautiful. And sweet. I . . . well, thank you, honey."

Yes! Finally, Jazz felt like she'd done something right. "You're welcome."

"And I'm really sorry I can't be at your art show. If there's any way I can sneak over, though, I will."

Jazz nodded. Maybe it was working. Jazz felt the anger begin to seep out of her. If she could keep it up — doing "Christian" things — then maybe she could feel like this all the time. "It's okay. And at least Dad will be there." She'd talked to him when he'd called home Tuesday, and he'd said he couldn't wait to see her art show.

"Your father? He's not coming home until Saturday night, Jasmine."

Jazz's throat and chest tightened. "He said he was coming back tomorrow morning."

Her mother shook her head. "He called this morning. They didn't finish with their sales conference, I guess."

"So he won't be there either?" She couldn't believe this. No, she *could* believe it. When would she ever learn? Why did she bother setting herself up like this? "Neither of you will be there?"

"You're shouting, Jasmine. Calm down."

Calm down? Calm down! That's what she'd been trying to do. A lot of good it had done her. Jazz turned and ran back to her room. Every ounce of anger had returned, multiplied.

I will not be angry! she told herself. But she knew her promises to herself weren't worth anything. It was like writing words in the sand. The first good wave wiped them out.

Jazz grabbed up her "do list," and threw herself onto her bed. She scratched her marker through "Mother." The marker she'd picked up was red. Ironic that it would be the same color that started this whole mess. The image of her little sister standing over the canvases, red paint dripping from her brush, rushed to Jazz's mind. And with it came that original anger.

How could she still be angry with Kendra? It wasn't Kendra's fault. And yet, every rotten thing that had happened in the last week had happened because Kendra destroyed those paintings.

The rest of the day, Jazz worked on removing paint from her self-portrait. When she was finished, she wrapped up all three paintings and walked them to Farley's Frames. She hung around until after closing to watch him frame the pictures. He didn't talk much, and she was glad. Jazz knew she should have been totally excited about tomorrow and her one-woman art show. But like everything else in her life that she "should have been," she wasn't.

Friday morning, Jazz woke up, and her first thought was of her one-woman show. But before she could enjoy that thought, another one clamored for attention. Kendra.

Jazz couldn't stand things not being right between them. She and her sister had always been close, no matter what else had gone on around them. She had to make things right with Kendra.

If she could just convince Kendra that she wasn't angry with her anymore... Everything Jazz thought of doing for her sister seemed lame, even to her. What she needed was a peace offering, a sign, a proof that she wasn't angry. But what could she give to Kendra?

Then she got it. Last year they'd gone to a street fair in Big Lake, and Jazz had won a purple bear. Kendra had wanted it in the worst way, but Jazz needed it because the color was one she wanted for a painting she'd been working on at school. She hadn't been able to mix up the color that was in her head until she saw that bear. So instead, Jazz had played game after game, trying to win another purple bear for her sister. She'd won a brown bear, a red bear, a purple turtle, and a couple of other prizes. She'd given them all to Kendra, but deep down, she'd known Kendra had still wanted that purple bear.

It took Jazz over an hour to find the stupid bear, but she finally discovered it stuffed on the top shelf of a downstairs closet. She could hardly wait to give it to her sister. Jazz tore upstairs, knocked on Kendra's door, and went on in. "Kendra, I've got something for you!" She hid the bear behind her back.

"You don't need to got me something," Kendra said. She was sitting on her bed, drawing in a notebook.

"But I wanted to." Jazz pulled the bear from behind her back. "Remember? Remember how much you wanted this bear last year at the fair?"

Kendra smiled and nodded her head, but she didn't get as excited as Jazz thought she would. "That's your bear. You need that color."

"Not anymore. Here! I want you to have it." She held out the bear to Kendra.

Kendra stayed where she was. She didn't reach for the bear. "That's okay, Jasmine."

"Take it!" Jazz heard the edge in her voice. She couldn't believe Kendra wouldn't want the bear. She'd moped around for days after the fair.

"It's a nice bear. Thank you. But it doesn't help," Kendra said softly. "You're still mad at me."

"Kendra, I'm telling you I'm not angry anymore! I'm giving you my bear. You're as bad as Ty and Mother and everybody else. I'm really trying to do better. Just tell me what to do? What more can I do?"

Kendra put down her pencil and squinted her small, almond-shaped eyes at Jazz. "It's not a *do* thing. It's a *be* thing."

The rest of the day Jazz tried to put everything out of her mind except her own art show. When she heard Ty and Kendra practicing Kendra's line for the play, she turned up her music. Mick came over, and Ty and Kendra helped her bake cookies to take to the church for after the play. Still, Jazz stayed in her room alone.

When it was time for Jazz to get ready for the art show, she must have tried on a dozen outfits. Nothing felt right. Finally, she called Storm to see what she was going to wear.

"Me?" Storm asked. The question was followed by silence, something that didn't happen often around Storm Novelo. "Jazz, I promised Kendra I'd see her in her play tonight."

Jazz didn't answer right away. She knew Annie, and Grace, and Mick would go to their church's play. She'd just assumed Storm would be with her at the art show. "I see."

"I thought Kendra would have told you. Jazz, she really wants you to be there too."

The words hung between them. "Kendra knows I have the art show," Jazz said. "She doesn't expect me to miss my own art show, does she?"

"I didn't say she expected you to go to her play. I just said she wanted you to."

This wasn't fair. Jazz shouldn't have to feel guilty for attending her own art show, especially since nobody else in her family and none of her friends were going to be there. *They* should be the ones feeling guilty. "Kendra won't even notice I'm not there." She tried to make her voice light, happy. "She'll have all of you guys in her cheering section."

Jazz got dressed, but it was still too early to go to Farley's Frames. Since she couldn't think of anything else to do to pass the time, she logged onto *That's What You Think!*

She started reading, but never made it past the verse Mick had posted at the top of the blog:

> *For it is by grace you have been saved, through faith — and this not from yourselves, it is the gift of God — not by works, so that no one can boast.*
>
> —Ephesians 2:8–9

Jazz read it over and over, trying to drink in the words. *Not from yourselves . . . not by works . . .* In those words, Jazz could hear Kendra's words: "It's not a *do* thing. It's a *be* thing."

Jazz's whole strategy had been to *do* Christian things. Works. That's how she'd wanted to get peace. Why wouldn't God let her earn this close friendship with him?

The answer was there. Because everybody could boast about it. But it was more than that. Gracie's blog about paying for sin had made more sense than Jazz had wanted to admit. Nobody had to prove to her that she was messed up. She needed someone to pay for all the things she'd said and done and thought. She couldn't do that herself. She hadn't even been able to get rid of her anger on her own.

"We're going, Jazz." Ty stood in the doorway with Kendra by his side. She was carrying a plate of cookies, and so was he.

A horn honked.

"That's the church bus," Ty said. "Come on, Kendra."

But Kendra didn't move. She stared at Jazz. "Would you come, Jazz?"

Jazz couldn't look away. She had never felt more torn in her whole life.

"Please?" Kendra begged.

"She's going to her art show," Ty said, tugging on Kendra's elbow, pulling her toward the stairs.

Jazz followed them. She followed them down the steps and out the front door. She kept walking behind them as they headed for the old brown church bus. Through the windows, Jazz could see Gracie, Storm, Mick, and Annie seated in the bus.

Hamlet, Gracie's blog name for their English teacher, was driving. "All aboard!" he shouted, revving the engine.

Ty jumped on.

Kendra turned and stared at Jazz. Jazz thought her heart would split in two. Then Kendra wrapped her chubby hand around the door rail and pulled herself up into the bus.

Storm stuck out her head before Hamlet could close the bus door. "Jasmine Fletcher! Get on in here and come see this play with us. You know you want to!"

Part of Jazz did want to. She wanted to see Kendra in the play. She wanted to be with her friends. But that wasn't what she wanted most. She wanted peace. And she knew now she'd never have it if she didn't turn her life over to Jesus and let him give it to her.

But another part of Jazz couldn't imagine turning her back on her own one-woman art show. Wasn't *that* the most important thing in her life? Wasn't it?

Gracie and Mick had their faces pressed against the window. Annie opened her window and shouted out, "Come on, Jazz!"

"I . . . I can't decide!" Jazz cried. She was standing a foot from the door to the bus, hearing the hiss of the door as it started to close.

Gracie managed to pull down her bus window and shout out, "If you don't come, that's deciding, Jazz! You'll be here. We'll be there."

The doors were closing.

"But I don't have anything to bring!" Jazz shouted, remembering the cookies.

This time it was Mick who yelled out the window. "Don't you get it, Jazz? You can't bring anything to this one!"

Jazz understood. It made sense. What did she have to bring to Christ, except all that anger and frustration?

But the bus doors were shutting. She was too late. "Wait!" she cried.

A hand appeared through the slit between the closing bus doors. A chubby hand. The doors swished open again.

"Jump!" Kendra screamed. "Jump, Jazz!"

Jazz took a deep breath and jumped.

She heard the cheers as she flew over the curb and into the bus. She had no idea if they knew what she'd just done. Jazz wasn't just jumping into a church bus. She felt as if she were jumping off a cliff. And when she landed, she landed in the open arms of Jesus.

14

It was a noisy, bumpy ride to church. Jazz sat squished between Storm and Kendra. But she thought she'd never enjoyed a ride as much as she did this one. She didn't say much, but she soaked it all in. And as she did, her anger broke apart, replaced by something else, something new.

Once in the church, Storm managed to wrangle front-row seats for all of the blog team. Annie helped her mom backstage, and the play began. Act One took place the Sunday before Easter, with Jesus riding into Jerusalem. Kendra got to cheer and wave a palm branch. Jazz watched in awe as the play took them through that week up to the Last Supper. She heard the verse about Jesus giving them a peace that the world couldn't, and she smiled to herself. She understood now.

She watched as they acted out Jesus' arrest, the beatings, the crucifixion and death. Kendra was crying in the back of the crowd. She shouted her line, "They can't do this to Jesus!" Jazz didn't think anyone could have asked for a better weeping woman than Kendra.

But the last act was the best. The audience grew noisy, with everyone getting in on the "Hallelujahs!" when Jesus rose from the dead and went back to heaven. And Jazz felt a part of it all.

She was scoping the stage for sight of Kendra when the microphone squeaked and Kendra appeared front and center.

"What's she doing?" Jazz asked Ty, panicked.

Ty shrugged and asked Mick, but Mick had no idea.

"Ladies and gentleman!" A man stood next to Kendra, holding the microphone between them. "One of our weeping ladies, Kendra Fletcher, has something to say."

Jazz's heart pounded. Sometimes Kendra could start talking about things that had nothing to do with anything going on around her.

"Instead of eating cookies here, you should come to..." She turned and said something to the man beside her. Then she turned back. "Farmies!" she shouted.

"Right," the man said. "Farley's Frames. Because..."

"Because my sister is an artist there!" Kendra finished.

Somehow, everybody must have understood Kendra's message because they all showed up at Farley's Frames, or at least enough to fill the shop. Jazz held Kendra's hand as they moved from one painting to the next, listening to praise of Jazz's original artwork.

They stopped in front of the abstract, where the smallest crowd had gathered. A woman Jazz had never seen before frowned at the painting. "It's so angry."

Jazz had to smile. The woman was right. The painting *was* angry.

But Kendra stepped up to Jazz's defense. "You shouldn't say that."

The woman smiled down at Kendra. "I'm sorry. I didn't mean anything by it. I do like the painting. In fact, I'm thinking of buying it."

Jazz couldn't believe it. "Did you hear that, Kendra?" she whispered as they backed away from the painting. "That woman wants to buy my abstract!"

Kendra didn't seem excited about that, though. She was staring at Jazz. Then she smiled. It was her best, big-tooth, total-face smile. "Know what?"

"What, honey?"

"You're not mad at me anymore."

Jazz pulled Kendra to her and hugged her. Kendra was right. The anger Jazz had tried so hard to get rid of was gone. Jazz didn't kid herself. She'd had a lot of anger for a very long time. It would probably come back now and then. But the difference would be that from now on, she knew what to do with it. She knew where to go for peace. Maybe she couldn't control her anger, but she knew Christ could.

"No," she said, still clinging to Kendra. "I'm not angry anymore."

The blog team closed in around her, jostling each other and laughing. In spite of herself, Jazz felt a silly grin rise to her lips.

"What are you grinning about?" Gracie the Observer asked.

Storm stared up into Jazz's face. "What did you do, Jazz?" she asked, sounding suspicious.

Jazz elbowed Kendra and answered, "You guys, haven't you heard? It's not a *do* thing. It's a *be* thing."

Internet Safety by Michaela

People aren't always what they seem at first, like wolves in sheep's clothing. Chat rooms, blogs, and other places online can be fun ways to meet all kinds of people with all kinds of interests. But be aware and cautious. Here are some tips to help keep you safe while surfing the web, keeping a blog, chatting online, and writing e-mails.

- Never give out personal information such as your address, phone number, parents' work addresses or phone numbers, or the name and address of your school without your parents' or guardian's permission. It's okay to talk about your likes and dislikes, but keep private information just that—private.
- Before you agree to meet someone in person, first check with your parents or guardian to make sure it's okay. A safe way to meet for the first time is to bring a parent or guardian with you.
- You might be tempted to send a picture of yourself to new friends you've met online. Just in case your acquaintance is not who you think they are, check with your parent or guardian before you hit send.
- If you feel uncomfortable by angry, threatening, or other types of e-mails or posts addressed to you, tell your parent or guardian immediately.
- Before you promise to call a new friend on the telephone, talk to your parent or guardian first.
- Remember that just because you might read about something or someone online doesn't mean the information is true. Sometimes people say cruel or untruthful things just to be mean.
- If someone writes creepy posts, report him or her to the blog or website owner.

Following these tips will help keep you safe while you hang out online. If you're careful, you can learn a lot and meet tons of new people.

Subject: Michaela Jenkins

Age: 13 on May 19, 7th grade at Big Lake Middle School
Hair/Eyes: Dark brown hair/Brown eyes
Height: 5'

"Mick the Munch" is content and rooted in her relationship with Christ. She lives with her stepsis, Grace Doe, in the blended family of Gracie's dad and Mick's mom. She's a tomboy, an avid Cleveland Indians fan, and the only girl on her school's baseball team. A computer whiz, Mick keeps *That's What You Think!* up and running. She also helps out at Sam's Sammich Shop and manages to show her friends what deep faith looks like.

Subject: Grace Doe

Age: 15 on August 19, sophomore
Hair/Eyes: Blonde hair/Hazel eyes
Height: 5′ 5″

Grace doesn't think she is cute at all. The word "average" was meant for her. She dresses in neutral colors and camouflage to blend in. Grace does not wear makeup. She prefers to observe life rather than participate in it. A bagger at a grocery store, only her close friends and family can get away with calling her "Gracie." She is part of a blended family and lives with her dad and stepmom, two stepsiblings, and two half brothers. Her mother's job frequently keeps her out of town.

Subject: Annie Lind

Age: 16 on October 1, sophomore
Hair/Eyes: Auburn hair/Blue eyes
Height: 5′ 10″

Annie desperately wants guys to admire and like her. She is boy-crazy and thinks she always has to be in love. She considers herself to be an expert in matters of the heart. Annie takes being popular for granted because she has always been well-liked. She loves and admires her mom. Her dad was killed in a plane crash when Annie was two months old. Annie helps out at Sam's Sammich Shop, her mom's restaurant. She can be self-centered, though without being selfish.

Subject: Jasmine Fletcher

Age: 15 on July 13, freshman
Hair/Eyes: Black hair/Brown eyes
Height: 5' 6"

Jasmine is an artist who feels that no one, especially her art teacher and parents, understands her art. She is African American, and has great fashion sense, without being trendy. Her parents are quite well-to-do, and they won't let Jasmine get a job. She has a younger brother and a sister who has Down syndrome. She also had a brother who was killed in a drive-by shooting in the old neighborhood when Jazz was one.

Subject: Storm Novello

Age: 14 on September 1, freshman
Hair/Eyes: Brown hair/Dark brown eyes
Height: 5' 2"

Storm doesn't realize how pretty she is. She wishes she had blonde hair. She is Mayan/Mestisa, and claims to be a Mayan princess. Storm always needs to be the center of attention and doesn't let on how smart she is. She dresses in bright, flouncy clothing, and wears too much makeup. Storm is a completely different person around her parents. She changes into her clothes and puts her makeup on after leaving for school. Her parents are very loving, though they have little money.

Here's a sneak preview of the next book in the Faithgirlz! Blog On series.

1

I forgot!

Storm Novelo bolted straight up in bed. Her thoughts were spinning too fast for her to grab onto them. She'd forgotten *something*. She was sure of that.

She struggled to line up the facts. Storm was all about facts. For example, today was the day after Memorial Day. *Fact*: Memorial Day was first called Decoration Day. *Fact*: Since World War I, it has also been called Poppy Day.

No help there.

Storm shoved her long, straight black hair out of her face and squinted at the morning light peeking through her window. What was she forgetting? Homework? Only nine school days left in the year. Nine more days as a freshman at Big Lake High School. Four of the days were makeups because Big Lake, Ohio, had used up all its snow days by early January.

But Storm would never feel this kind of panic over homework.

She yawned. If she could just go back to sleep ...

No way. Storm couldn't shake the feeling that she'd forgotten something major. It was more than a feeling. Close to a fact. A subconscious fact. Hadn't she just read last week that most memory lies in the subconscious? It was a great article too. About how seven items can pass through the gate of a person's short-term memory, but if you add the eighth, it's too much. And how even for seven items, the subconscious stores them better with a system, like memory hooks or mnemonics. Like remembering the colors in the rainbow as "Roy G. Biv," for red, orange, yellow, green, blue, indigo, violet.

This was so not helping.

What had she forgotten?

Her blog? Storm was part of a blogging team made up of her best friends. They worked together on a website called *That's What You Think!* She'd promised Gracie, their chief blogger, that she'd have her trivia column written by this afternoon's blog meeting. She didn't have it yet, but she would. Trivia came easily to Storm Novelo. So that wasn't it.

Then she got it. "The Mexican hat plant!"

Bounding out of bed, she raced for the door. Her shin slammed into her mother's sewing machine. "Ow!"

She pressed on, shoving aside the maze of clothes hanging like drapes all around the tiny room. Storm's bedroom served as her mother's sewing room. Since Mom had taken the customer-service job at the supermarket, the turnaround on mending jobs had gotten longer. More and more clothes kept piling up.

Storm flung open the bedroom door and dashed to the kitchen.

Her mother set down the teakettle. "Storm? What's the matter?"

"I forgot!" Storm cried, crossing the kitchen for the little makeshift greenhouse. "Dad's plant! I forgot to bring it in last night."

"Oh, Storm." Her mother didn't need to say more. Her tone said it all. Storm's father did not need this.

Bringing in that plant was the only thing Dad had asked her to do for him. He'd babied his Mexican hat plant for months. That plant was just about the only thing he'd shown interest in for weeks. He'd carried the planter from the yard to the greenhouse and back again dozens of times, depending on the forecast.

But Memorial Day was his busiest day of the whole year, the day he had to make sure the cemetery lawns stayed groomed and clean. So he'd asked Storm to see to his plant. When he'd left for the cemetery, he'd reminded her to bring in the hat plant because the forecast called for severe thunderstorms, possibly mixed with hail. For once, the weathermen had gotten it right.

Storm and her blogging buddies had spent the evening eating ice cream at Sam's Sammich Shop, the local hangout owned by Samantha Lind. Annie Lind, Sam's daughter, had driven everybody home when it started to sprinkle. Storm had been dropped off last, and the sky had opened just as she stepped out of Annie's car. She'd had to run through giant raindrops mixed with tiny ice pellets.

And still she'd forgotten all about Dad's plant.

Storm slid on the waxed kitchen linoleum as she made the turn into the tiny greenhouse. It smelled like a jungle — musty, but fresh. Her dad had built it himself out of plastic and used lumber. The greenhouse opened onto their small backyard.

There in the corner of the yard stood Storm's dad, his back toward her. He was leaning over what was left of his favorite plant.

Dear God, Storm prayed, wishing she'd thought to pray sooner, *please make Dad's plant be okay. Make* me *be okay too, while you're at it.* Storm was still new at being a Christian, and she didn't think she was a very good one yet. If she had been, she wouldn't have forgotten something that meant so much to her dad, especially when he was like this.

Storm hadn't seen her dad this depressed since they'd made the move to Ohio. As far as she could tell, the depression had crept up on him, beginning a few weeks ago and gripping him tighter every day.

And now she'd done this, making everything worse.

Mud squished through her toes as she made her way to the back of the yard. Her dad didn't turn around. He showed no sign of knowing she was there. Instead, Eduardo Novelo stared into the white planter, his back bent sideways at exactly the same angle as the scraggly plant, as if the night's storm had been too much for both of them.

"Dad, I'm so sorry."

He didn't move. He didn't look at her.

"I didn't mean to leave it outside. I got back late. And I just forgot." Her excuse sounded lame, even to her. "I should have brought it in before I went out." She wanted him to turn around, to yell at her. Shout. Scream. Anything would be better than this silence.

"Dad?" She took another step closer. "Will you forgive me? Can I do something to make it up to you? I'll work extra hours at the supermarket, okay? I can earn enough money to buy another plant just like this one." She tried to remember what he'd said about the plant. He called it a Mexican hat plant, but it had other names, like mother of thousands, and a longer name she couldn't remember. She thought he'd ordered it from somewhere down South.

Without looking at her, he said, "It is my fault. I was a fool to try."

"To try what? To try to grow it here?" Storm asked. Sometimes she had to answer her own questions when he was like this. "Why? Because it's too cold in Ohio? Too wet?"

It was a long time before he spoke. Storm waited because she didn't know what else to do. "In Texas," he began, his voice barely above a whisper, "it grows like a cactus flower. I just thought ..."

"You thought you could grow it in the greenhouse," Storm said, finishing his sentence because he didn't seem to have the strength to finish it himself.

"In Florida," he continued, "it grows so freely that some think it is a weed."

Storm knew that even if everybody else in the whole world considered that plant a weed, her dad didn't. He called dandelions flowers. If dandelions didn't grow so easily, he insisted, they would be considered rare and beautiful flowers. Although he pulled them out of other people's yards, he took great care to grow them in his own yard. He'd cultivated dandelions to frame their whole backyard. She glanced around at the dandelions and was surprised to see how overgrown everything looked.

"It doesn't matter," he said, finally.

But it did matter. Storm knew it did, as much as anything could matter to her dad now. What she didn't understand was why it mattered so much. "Is the flower from Mexico?" she asked. There had been two blooms on the plant before the storm, and they really did look like Mexican hats, with tall centers and low petals that made the brim of a hat.

Her father shook his head. Storm caught a glimpse of his face, wrinkled and brown from hours in the sun doing yard work for rich people. "The flower comes from Madagascar," he said softly.

"But your parents grew them when you were a boy, right?" She was in dangerous territory now. She could almost see her dad growing smaller, sinking into himself. Her dad's mother had died before Storm was born. His father, Storm's only living grandparent, had never visited them. And they had never gone to Chicago to see him, at least not that Storm remembered. He'd remarried and had a whole new family now.

"I should have kept the plant in the greenhouse," her dad said. He'd turned his back on Storm again, so it sounded like he was talking to the leafless stalk of a plant. "I just wanted it to see the sun."

"Time for breakfast!" Storm's mother called from the kitchen, her voice loud and clear through the kitchen window.

Storm waited for her dad, but he didn't seem to hear. Usually, whenever Storm's mother called, her dad hopped to it. Tina Novelo was small, like Storm, not much over five feet and not a pound over one hundred. But she had an air of authority and strength about her. Storm's dad called her his Mayan princess.

Storm touched her dad's arm. "Dad? We better — "

"Storm, you'll be late for school!" her mother shouted.

Storm started to say something to her dad, then gave up and walked inside. She wasn't hungry, but she sat at the kitchen table anyway. "Won't Dad even come in for breakfast?" she asked.

Her mother poured hot water into an old teacup, the cream paint cracked and stained. "Your father isn't hungry."

Storm hadn't seen her dad eat in three days, but she didn't question her mom. Her parents knew each other too well. They'd had a secret language her whole life, a way of communicating without words. Her mom knew her dad better than Storm would ever know either one of them.

"Why is he acting like this?" Storm asked, sipping the orange juice set on the table for her. There were three glasses of juice set out. A full Spanish omelet sat waiting in the pan on the stove. Maybe Tina Novelo didn't know her husband as well as she thought she did.

"Your father is depressed. You know that."

"But why? I don't know why."

Her mother sat down at the small kitchen table. "There's not always a *why* to know."

Storm waited for more, but she didn't get it. Finally, she went to her room and got dressed for school. She chose bright yellow — a yellow peasant blouse and a yellow peasant skirt. She reached for her yellow flowered sandals, the ones she'd bought at a garage sale for a dollar. Then she thought better of it. Why wear a built-in reminder of the flower disaster?

Storm studied herself in the mirror as she swept up her straight hair into a ponytail. She'd hoped bright yellow would change her mood. But so far, it wasn't working. She couldn't get the picture out of her head, the image of her dad slumping like the wind-broken stem.

faiThGirLz!™

2 corinthians 4:18

Inner Beauty, Outward Faith

Grace Notes

Softcover • ISBN 0-310-71093-6

Grace, a loner by nature, prefers blogging anonymously about her high school classmates to befriending them. But when a new student discovers Grace's identity, both girls are forced to reconsider their status as outsiders. Will Grace choose to have a wonderful new friend—or will she keep her distance?

Love, Annie

Softcover • ISBN 0-310-71094-4

Annie Lind was born to be "Professor Love," her website column for the lovelorn. She knows how to handle guys! When her dream date asks her out, she thinks she's in love—and neglects her friends and commitments. It'll take some guidance from an unexpected source to teach her what real love is.

Just Jazz

Softcover • ISBN 0-310-71095-2

Jazz is working on a masterpiece: herself... Jasmine "Jazz" Fletcher is an artist down to her toes; she sees beauty and art where others see nothing. And her work on the website is drawing rave reviews. But if she doesn't come up with a commercially successful masterpiece pretty soon, her parents may make her drop what they consider an expensive hobby to focus on a real job.

Storm Rising

Softcover • ISBN 0-310-71096-0

Nobody knows the real Storm... not even Storm! The center of attention wherever she goes, Storm Novelo is impetuous, daring, loud—and a phony. Convinced that no one would like her inner brainiac, she hides her genius behind her public airhead.

Available now at your local bookstore!

faiThGirLz!™
2 corinthians 4:18

Inner Beauty, Outward Faith

Grace Under Pressure

Softcover • ISBN 0-310-71263-7

Gracie's always been good at handling everything herself, but pressures at school and personal disappointments prove almost more than she can bear in this fifth book in the Blog On series. Will she learn to share her burdens with God and with her friends before she cracks?

Upsetting Annie

Softcover • ISBN 0-310-71264-5

Annie has a great life. She loves her girlfriends, never lacks for guy friends, and she's a cheerleader too. But her confidence is shaken when her cousin from Paris, France, moves in. Shawna is funny, cute, and a talented cheerleader. Soon Shawna is the center of attention— and Annie's not. How can she banish jealousy before it ruins her life?

Storm Warning

Softcover • ISBN 0-310-71266-1

Storm Novelo was sure that once she became a Christian, she'd be ... well, perfect. But she's not. She can't even manage to be civil to the arrogant Cameron Worthington III at school. What's more, her dad is suffering from depression, and her mistakes only seem to make matters worse. Will she ever be able to make him proud of her?

Available now at your local bookstore

Inner Beauty, Outward Faith

Book 1 **Sophie's World** . . . . Softcover . . . ISBN 0-310-70756-0
Book 2 **Sophie's Secret** . . . . Softcover . . . ISBN 0-310-70757-9
Book 3 **Sophie and the Scoundrels** . Softcover . . . ISBN 0-310-70758-7
Book 4 **Sophie's Irish Showdown** . . . Softcover . . . ISBN 0-310-70759-5
Book 5 **Sophie's First Dance?** . . . . . . Softcover . . . ISBN 0-310-70760-9
Book 6 **Sophie's Stormy Summer** . . . Softcover . . . ISBN 0-310-70761-7
Book 7 **Sophie Breaks the Code** . . . . Softcover . . . ISBN 0-310-71022-7
Book 8 **Sophie Tracks a Thief** . . . . . . Softcover . . . ISBN 0-310-71023-5
Book 9 **Sophie Flakes Out** . . . . Softcover . . . ISBN 0-310-71024-3
Book 10 **Sophie Loves Jimmy** . . . . Softcover . . . ISBN 0-310-71025-1
Book 11 **Sophie Loses the Lead** . . . . . Softcover . . . ISBN 0-310-71026-X
Book 12 **Sophie's Encore** . . . . Softcover . . . ISBN 0-310-71027-8

Available now at your local bookstore!

ZONDERkidz™

Faithgirlz! Journal

Spiral • ISBN 0-310-71190-8

The questions in this new Faithgirlz!™ journal focus on your life, family, friends, and future. Because your favorites and issues seem to change every day, the same set of questions are repeated in each section. Includes quizzes to promote reflection and stickers to add fun!

NIV Faithgirlz! Backpack Bible

Periwinkle Italian Duo-Tone™ • ISBN 0-310-71012-X

The full NIV text in a handy size for girls on the go—for ages 8 and up.

Inner Beauty, Outward Faith

Visit **faithgirlz.com**—
it's the place for girls ages 8-12!